Dancers

Sand Dancers

Blue Moon
Ballet

Lynda Waterhouse

PICCADILLY PRESS • LONDON

For my mum, Aline Waterhouse

First published in Great Britain in 2010
by Piccadilly Press Ltd,
5 Castle Road, London NW1 8PR
www.piccadillypress.co.uk

A catalogue record for this book is available from the British Library

ISBN: 978 1 84812 065 5 (paperback)

1 3 5 7 9 10 8 6 4 2

Printed in the UK by CPI Bookmarque Ltd, Croydon, CR0 4RD
Cover design by Simon Davis
Cover illustration by Sue Hellard

Mixed Sources
Product group from well-managed
forests and other controlled sources
www.fsc.org Cert no. TT-COC-002227
© 1996 Forest Stewardship Council
FSC

Extract from *The Book of Faeries and Other Strange Creatures* by Nathaniel Relyveld, 1847:

The Sand Sprites

Little is known about these mysterious creatures apart from the fact that they live inside sand dunes and follow the rules set down in the ancient book, *The Sands of Time*. They are winged creatures that have lost the ability to fly.

Male sand sprites are known as sand farers, and spend long periods of time travelling the deserts of the world in sand galleons, or go to sea. Young males are known as surf boys. They spend their time learning the ways of the sea, preparing to be sand farers.

Female sand sprites either sift the sand to keep it pure, or those with the most talent for dancing become sand dancers. Sand dancers train for many a long year until they can perform the secret dune dances. Their feelings run deep and, when thwarted, they can bear a grudge.

Let us not forget the ancient belief that if they stop dancing then disaster will strike the earth.

Chapter One

'Hope is like a strong wind;
it can carry a grain of sand over thousands of miles.'
The Sands of Time

Cassandra Marramgrass scanned the horizon excitedly as the dune bug she was travelling on edged its way towards Dreamy Dune. She hugged her box of dancing slippers, shook her sandy-blond braids from her face and whispered, 'Sparkling sea horses!' All her happy feelings burst out of her, making her tiny wings twitch and tingle.

'This term I am going to practise and practise. I am going to become a great sand dancer,' she promised herself.

In a few twists of the sand timer, she and all the other young sand dancers that were crammed on top of the dune bug – partly because of space, and partly to keep warm in the winter weather – would be arriving to start their second term at the Sandringham Dance School.

It was such a delightful thought that she couldn't stop herself from calling out, 'Seven sparkling sea horses swimming in a shiny sea!'

Some of the other sprites giggled and one or two looked at her disapprovingly, but Cassie was far too happy to care. She could see Sandringham now, a tiny speck in the distance, and she would soon be there.

I wonder if Shell and Lexie have already arrived, she thought. She was so looking forward to catching up with her best friends after the three-week holiday she'd spent at Mite Cove with only her Aunt Euphorbia for company. She longed for Shell to make her laugh as usual and to hear Lexie's kind words of encouragement. She had been disappointed to find they weren't on her dune bug.

Cassie could hardly believe that before last term she had actually hated dancing and she had only auditioned for the dancing school in order to find out more about her mother, the famous prima dune dancer, Marina Marramgrass. Marina had disappeared just over seven years before during the Night of the Great Sandstorm, and Cassie had been desperate to find out what had happened to her, and why she had visited the dance school just before she disappeared.

After some snooping, Cassie had found out that Sandrine, the Supreme Sand Sprite, had sent Marina on a very important mission. There were many reports that the dunes around the world were slowly being destroyed, but that dance could prevent this from happening. Sandrine had ordered her very best sand dancer, Marina, to visit all the sand dunes and discover which local dances were the most powerful. These dances were then going to be put together to create a dune dance so wonderful, it was hoped, that it would not only stop the destruction of the dunes, but restore them to health and make them sing again.

But just as Marina had started on this important journey, their land had been struck by a terrible sandstorm, which had caused much death and destruction. There had been no word from her since. At the end of last term, though, there was news! Marina had been spotted on a faraway dune and a search party had been sent to find her. One of those in the party was Cassie's best friend, the surf boy Rubus.

But all this was secret – hardly any sprites knew what Marina's quest had been, or that there was any recent news of her. Even the serious state of the dunes was known by only a few sprites – for fear of causing panic, Cassie supposed. After the Great Sandstorm, the dance school had been closed while all the sand sprites concentrated on repairing their damaged land. Now the school had reopened, and it was time to start dancing again.

* * *

The dune bug seemed to be taking ages to cover the last stretch of sand. Cassie looked out at Dreamy Dune, growing larger as they slowly approached. Everything looked the same – the large mountains of sand and the tall wind-swept grasses. Cassie took a deep breath of cold icy air. There was the same tangy smell of sea and sand crystals. And yet one of her teachers, clever Miss Youngsand Jnr, had discovered that the natural world around them was changing and dance steps needed to be taken to help save it from disappearing.

Cassie sighed and shook her braids. *Sandrine, the Supreme Sand Sprite will sort things out with help from the sand dancers,* she thought. *And when my mother returns with the collection of dance steps from all the dunes of the world, we will work hard to combine them into one powerful dance so things will get better. In the meantime, I have to stay out of trouble, work hard and concentrate on my dancing.*

The dune bug suddenly lurched to one side, inter-rupting her thoughts, and forcing all the sprites to cling on to their bags and boxes. The bug righted itself, but after three steps it lurched in the other direction. Cassie's bag slipped and, as she reached to save it, the bag tipped over, spilling sand cakes and a slim package. Cassie just managed to grab hold of the package, but the sand cakes bounced and rolled down the side of Dreamy Dune.

'Are you all right, Cassie?' her friend Ella asked. 'Only

you keep wriggling and sighing. Have you got cramp and need to stretch?'

Cassie laughed. Ella might be one of the smallest and youngest sand dancers, but what she lacked in age she made up for in talent and curiosity. 'My sand cakes are now on their way back to Mite Cove!' explained Cassie, pointing at them.

'That's a shame,' Ella said. 'Were you too excited to eat them earlier?'

Cassie nodded. 'My tummy has been fluttering with excitement since this morning.'

'Mine too. I can't wait to get back. This term we might even learn some of the secret dune dances. We were so lucky to win places at the school, weren't we? I still keep pinching myself when I think about it, just to see if I'm dreaming.' Ella giggled. 'Do you remember how homesick I was at first and how much I blubbed?'

'You poor shrimp! Well, you are one of the youngest here,' Cassie teased.

'You and Shell and Lexie were so kind to me, taking me under your wings. It's such a shame that Lexie won't be coming back straight away, isn't it?'

'What do you mean?' Cassie gasped. 'Lexie's not coming back straight away? Is it her leg?'

Lexie had fallen over sand boarding at the end of the previous term and Cassie still felt a bit responsible for encouraging her to race in the first place. Lexie was usually so quiet and sensible, but she got carried away sometimes, especially when encouraged by her friends.

Ella nodded. 'Yes. Apparently her leg swelled up and is really badly sprained. Madame Rosa insisted that she fully recover before she comes back. Madame Rosa stopped at our cove on her way back to Sandringham, so that's how I heard the news.'

'Will she be away for a long time?' Cassie asked, worried.

'I'm not sure. She'll come back when she's built up her strength, I suppose,' Ella replied.

'It won't be the same without Lexie.' Cassie felt sick with disappointment. It was hard to imagine dance school without her friend. Her excitement at being back faded, and she didn't join in with the loud cheer that went up when at last the dune bug mounted the crest of Dreamy Dune. The bug carried them down through the hidden doorway and stopped right at the front of the large mother-of-pearl gates of the Sandringham Dance School.

Thassalinus, the retired sand farer, opened the gates for them. He smiled when he saw Cassie and called out, 'Any news of that young whippersnapper, Rubus? Haven't seen him about these parts for a while.' Thassalinus licked his lips. 'Always brought me some barnacle beer. I haven't tasted a decent drop in a long while.'

Cassie shook her head and tried to answer lightly. 'I expect he's sand boarding or racing his sand sailing ship

8

somewhere.'

Thassalinus chuckled. 'Getting up to no good as usual.'

Cassie gave a weak smile back. She couldn't tell him where Rubus had really gone – that he was risking his life aboard a sand galleon to help find her mother and bring her home. Cassie hoped for the thousandth time that he was not in any danger.

There was a mad scramble to get off the dune bug, with bags flying and sand sprites jostling to be the first.

At the main entrance to the school, Calluna, the senior sand dancer, was waiting for them with a clipboard in her hand and a stern expression on her face. When the sprites saw her, they straightened themselves up. It was one of Calluna's responsibilities to see that all the sand dancers followed the Rules set out in the ancient book of the sand sprites, *The Sands of Time,* and she was very strict at enforcing them.

'Sand *dancers,* not scuttlers or prancers!' she called out. 'Line up sensibly, please, and let me check off your luggage and do the register and kutch allocations.'

Cassie stretched her legs and smoothed down her crumpled dress before joining the line.

As Calluna ticked her name off the list, she announced, 'Cassandra Marramgrass, you are in the same sleeping kutch.'

The previous term, Calluna had given Cassie what she thought was the worst kutch in the school – a dusty room at the very top of the school. But Cassie loved it, because it had a balcony with a ladder down to the beach, which meant she could always escape from the school when she needed to.

Cassie smiled at her. 'Thank you.' Then she asked, 'Did you have a good break?' She was determined to try and be friendly to Calluna. They had not got off to a good start when they first met, and sand sprites were known to bear grudges if they felt they had been slighted.

Calluna looked at her, blinking in surprise. 'No time for talking or you'll be late,' she replied sternly, but as Cassie turned to go she gave a sweet half-smile and added in a softer voice, 'It does feel good to be back.'

When she was sure that Calluna wouldn't see, she ran all the way up the stairs to the floor where all the other sleeping kutches were. From there, she climbed the rickety stepladder and skipped along the narrow passage to her kutch, pulled back the curtain and rushed inside. The floor smelled of fresh polish and the mother-of-pearl mirror had been given a shine, but apart from a new shelf above her bed, her kutch was just the same as ever.

She threw down her bag and her box of dancing slippers on the bed and rushed to open the peephole that led out to the balcony. She enjoyed the refreshing flutter of the sea breeze on her face. Before she knew it, her toes had started to wiggle and tap. Usually this meant a Rage Stomp, but this time they were tapping out a Glad Stamp.

'Rat a tap tap
I'm back, I'm back
Rat a tap tap
So glad, so glad
Rat a tap twirl
I smile and smile
Rat a tap twirl
As my wings unfurl!'

She swirled and twirled around every corner of her sleeping kutch, pointing her toes in one corner and gliding around another. As she bent over to pick up her bag, she performed a Dune Arabesque, stretching one leg out behind her and holding it as still as she could while she carefully unpacked the practice dress that her Aunt Euphorbia had made for her. It was salmon pink and each panel on the skirt was embroidered with flowers and plants that grew in the dunes near their home in Mite Cove.

Cassie held it up against her. Her aunt had let down some of the panels because she had grown, and it fitted perfectly. She put it to one side and took out the small package. It was a bit crumpled, but Cassie smoothed out the creases and carefully loosened the grass binding. Her aunt had wrapped her surprise going-away present really

11

well. Cassie dared not think about how close she had come to losing it. The parcel had three layers of delicate gossamer fabric and, as she untied the last layer, she uncovered a dainty shrug.

Cassie fingered the fine fabric. It was made up of lots of little knots and must have taken her aunt a very long time to finish. A lump came to her throat when she thought about her Aunt Euphorbia's twisted fingers struggling to make it for her after a hard day at the sand factory. Her aunt did not approve of dancing, often saying that it caused nothing but heartbreak, but she always made Cassie beautiful things to dance in. She also gave Cassie advice about dancing, even though she didn't know the first thing about it. The shrug was perfect, because it was warm and light so that she could wear it while she was dancing or slip it on over her practice dress after a class.

Finally, Cassie carefully took her dancing slippers out of the box. 'We are going to work so hard this term,' she whispered as she placed them alongside her exercises book on the small shelf above her bed.

'Are you ready yet? Or have you been turned into a sea slug and are lolling about in slime?' A familiar voice called up to her from the bottom of the rickety stepladder.

Cassie made her best sea-slug-gurgling-in-slime impression as Shell climbed up the stepladder. Shell had a wild and adventurous streak that was fun to be around, and very infectious. Like Lexie, Cassie had met Shell at the entry audition and they had all been friends ever since. Shell had secrets of her own to keep, and that made them even closer.

Cassie looked up at her friend and gasped. 'Galloping sea spiders! What have you done to your hair?'

Shell patted the two large coils of braids that were arranged around her ears and smiled proudly. 'It's the latest fashion at the palace. Don't you like it?'

Cassie was used to seeing her friend's hair in wide braids that flowed around her face. She frowned. 'I'm not sure. It's so different.'

'We all had to have them done when the Prince of Tides passed by for a visit. It's good to have something to help weigh you down when he drops in at the palace.'

Cassie's eyes twinkled with curiosity. 'The Prince of Tides! What's he *really* like? I've heard so many different stories about him. He is in charge of the surf boys, isn't he?'

Shell said, 'Yes, he ensures that they understand the flow of the tides and the science of the waves. They have to care about all sea life and be good at delivering messages, as you know. He only seems to have time for the strongest sprites – he can be very mean to sprites that he thinks are weak. Sandrine says that has always been a part of his nature ever since he was little, and she is his big sister so she should know.'

'I am not sure that I would like to meet him then,' Cassie said. 'What was the Prince of Tides doing at the palace?'

'He sometimes calls in unexpectedly when the wind is in the right direction. When he gets agitated, or even if he just laughs too loudly, rough sea spray slaps you in the face. You have to stay very still when he's around!'

'How did *you* manage that?' Cassie asked. Shell was not the type of sprite to sit quietly in the background. She expected to be the centre of attention. Shell was actually Anagallis, the Supreme Sand Sprite Sandrine's daughter. However, she did not want to be treated differently to anyone else at the dance school and so she kept her real identity secret – only Cassie and Lexie knew who she really was – and at Sandringham she pretended to be Shell, a serving sprite at the palace.

'With great difficulty, but,' Shell rolled her eyes, 'you'll be pleased to know that I have been having decorum lessons over the holidays.'

'Sounds painful,' Cassie commented. 'Have you heard about Lexie? That she won't be back right away? Her leg is still injured from the sand boarding contest and she needs to rest it.'

'Poor kid. She must be so frustrated not to be back with the rest of us. And who is going to help me with my sewing?' Shell pretended to look put out.

'All heart as usual,' Cassie laughed. Shell was hopeless at practical things like sewing or tidying up after herself.

'Just because I don't gush doesn't mean that I don't care. Let's go and have a walk before supper and see if anything's changed around here,' Shell suggested. 'I am feeling restless – it's so different here from being at the palace. It always takes me a while to get used to it.'

'Have you finished unpacking?' Cassie asked.

Shell chewed the side of her lip. 'Sort of. There are one or two things that I haven't done yet.'

Cassie laughed again. *One or two things* probably meant that there were several bags waiting to be unpacked. 'Come on,' she said, 'I'll help you and then we'll go and check out the rest of the school.'

'Great idea! I must show you my new practice dress. It's pale blue and embroidered with dog violets and the shade exactly matches the colour of my eyes. How clever is that!'

They smiled at each other. It was certainly good to be back.

Chapter Two

'It takes time and patience for the waves to polish a stone.'
The Sands of Time

They crept into the dining hall and gazed up at the large stained-glass window. It was made from pieces of glass that had been washed up on the beach and carefully sifted and saved by the sand sprites before being assembled into the window. Beams of sunlight stretched red, yellow and blue light to the floor. Cassie bathed her fingers in the light and said, 'This room really makes me feel that I belong to a great tradition of sand dancers.'

'This room makes me think about what's for supper,' Shell joked back.

They sniffed the air, trying to get a hint of what was going to be for dinner.

Cassie scrunched up her nose. 'It's definitely sea cucumber!'

'With a hint of wild thyme,' Shell agreed, sniffing deeply.

Cassie ran her fingers along the smooth driftwood tables. 'I was so excited about returning, but now that I'm back, I can't stop thinking about everything that I have to do, and I feel a bit grumpled.'

Grumpled was a strange mixture of sadness, happiness and crossness and Cassie always felt grumpled when she felt worried and overwhelmed by things.

'There is a lot of work to be done,' Shell agreed as she jumped up on to the raised platform where the teachers sat. She grabbed a napkin, wrapped it around her head, waggled a finger and said, 'Cassandra Marramgrass, I order you to stop feeling grumpled! Grumpled won't do a Sand Plié correctly and grumpled won't help your dancing one little bit!'

Cassie giggled at the impression, and performed an exaggerated curtsey. 'I hear and obey you, Mrs Sandskrit.'

'Good. Now go and fetch me ten sea pasties for I am a little peckish!' Shell ordered, rubbing her stomach.

'I am afraid I cannot,' Cassie said, 'for I have to meet my friend Shell in the Secrets Cupboard.'

'A Secrets Cupboard? Whatever next! Why, you'll be telling me that secret picnics are held or – horror – that some sand dancers actually dare to disobey the Rules and sneak out of the school!' Shell jumped down, linked arms with her friend and they Dart and Turned out of the room.

17

The Secrets Cupboard was actually an old, dusty stockroom which they sneaked into when they wanted to have private conversations.

When they walked inside this time, they found that all the shelves had been emptied and painted white. The cupboard had been completely cleared, apart from two large wicker baskets at the far end.

'It doesn't feel quite so secret now,' Cassie sighed with disappointment.

'A lot of the mystery has been cleared away,' Shell agreed as she opened one of the wicker baskets and wrinkled her nose. It released a sprinkling of dust into the air, before revealing old velvet curtains.

Cassie walked down to the end of the cupboard. 'Maybe this clean cupboard is a sign that sand sprites are changing and moving on . . . That we have recovered from the effects of the Night of the Great Sandstorm and we can talk freely about things.'

'And I thought it was just a place to come to chat with friends without being caught by Calluna or one of the teachers!' Shell said.

As they sat on the wicker baskets, Cassie wondered what secret talks and plans they would make in there this term.

'Let's check out the dance studio next!' Shell said, racing on ahead.

Cassie smiled after her friend. It must have been hard for Shell to behave herself at the palace, when all the time she wanted to be wild and free and dancing. Cassie felt the hairs prickle on the back of her neck and her tiny wings twitch. She felt certain that she was not alone.

She turned round quickly to see who was there, but the corridor was empty. There was just a faint odour of wet sand mixed with the tang of seaweed and brine with a hint of sea thyme.

Must be my mind playing tricks on me – or another sprite taking a sneaky peek and who doesn't want to get into trouble, she told herself as she ran to catch up with her friend.

'Did you see anyone else in the corridor?' she asked Shell as they opened the double doors that led into the practice room.

'Only the ghosts of past sand dancers frowning at me!' Shell pulled a spooky-looking face.

'Ha, ha, very funny,' Cassie said. They walked through the lobby with the benches and hooks where they hung their shoes, and into the studio. They both took a good look around the room. The walls were covered in mirrors and, although some of them were tarnished with age, someone had freshened up the paintwork around the edges. Cassie looked at the wooden floorboards and wondered how many other sprites had practised a Dart and Turn, or Sand Glide there for the floor to be so smooth.

'I can't wait to put on my practice dress and start dancing in here again,' Cassie said.

'What was that advice your Aunt Euphorbia gave you?' Shell asked.

'*You have to look the part to be the part*,' Cassie replied as they stared into the mirror, and, raising themselves up on the balls of their feet, they spontaneously chanted, 'Bend and stretch, bend and stretch – put some elasticity into your legs.'

Then they collapsed on to each other, giggling.

'Maybe when we do put on our practice dresses we will do better!' Shell sighed as she rubbed her legs. 'I am looking forward to classes starting up, but I am not looking forward to how stiff and achy I am going to feel afterwards.'

'We'll soon get used to it. Besides it's a different kind of ache when you know you are working towards being a sand dancer. The twinges are harder to get over after a shift at the sand factory.'

'Sift and stretch, sift and stretch, puts lots of twinges in Cassie's legs,' Shell sang as she mimed sifting sand.

'Last term we had the Harvest Moon Festival to look forward to. What do you think it will be like this term?' Cassie mused as she watched Shell check on her new hairstyle in the mirror.

'The problem with this style is that it gets lopsided too easily. You have to hold your head up straight all the time. This term should be a quiet one. I can handle nice and dull for a while. It would give me a chance to perfect the dance steps and sequences we learned last term.'

Cassie chewed her lip. 'I mustn't let myself be distracted by anything. I have to concentrate on improving my technique. I came very close to failing last term and I want to show Madame Rosa how determined I can be.'

Shell put an arm around her friend's shoulder. 'Don't be too hard on yourself, Cassie. We all had to adjust to being here last term and you were also trying to find out about your mother.'

Cassie half-smiled. 'Last term I didn't think there was any chance that I could ever become a good sand dancer, but now I know that it is possible I really want to do my best.'

Shell sighed. 'We will do our best, but we will absolutely have to have at least one midnight picnic. I get twitchy if I'm too well behaved for long.'

'Agreed,' said Cassie, nodding. 'We can't have you getting twitchy!'

They stared at each other in the mirrors. Shell struck a crazy twitchy pose. Cassie tried to smile, but instead her shoulders hunched sadly as she said, 'I want to have some fun too, but I have to work hard and improve for when . . .' She paused and swallowed.

'For when your mother returns,' Shell added softly.

Cassie nodded and tears sprang to her eyes.

'I can't imagine what it must be like meeting up with your mother after seven years apart. Sandrine was amazed at how much I had changed when she saw me after only a term away.'

Cassie swallowed back the tears and looked at her face in the mirror. It was hard for Cassie to hide her feelings as sand sprites were meant to. She looked down and said in a soft voice, 'I don't even know when she will be back. It wasn't that long ago I thought she might be dead and that I would never see her again. I have missed her so much, but sometimes I get really scared when I think about meeting her again.' She looked up at Shell's reflection in the mirror as she asked the question that had been playing on her mind. 'What if she doesn't like me?'

Shell winked. 'What's not to like?'

Cassie laughed. Shell's wicked sense of humour always made her feel better. They linked arms and walked out of the practice room and along the corridor.

'I got so bored and cross at the palace over the holidays. I know it sounds ungrateful and I am incredibly lucky to live there and have so many lovely things, but it was quite hard to get used to being Anagallis, daughter of the Supreme Sand Sprite, again. It seemed like someone was always around watching me and, believe it or not, I had got out of the habit of ordering sprites around.'

'That *is* hard to imagine,' Cassie replied, grinning.

Shell raised an eyebrow and continued. 'Then Sandrine hired Miss Lungwort to teach me Supreme Sand Sprite Decorum. I had to spend hours practising elaborate bows and nods and learning the correct way to get out of a dune bug. I have been zooming around in silver dune bugs and hoppers since I was a sand baby, but now when I have to do it I get knotted up with nerves, worrying that I am not using the right leg or bending my knees enough. Some days I was this far,' she held up her finger and thumb, 'from stealing a silver bug and racing down to Mite Cove to see you. Then I thought about the reception I would get from your Aunt Euphorbia and I changed my mind.'

Cassie laughed and furrowed her eyebrows. 'My aunt does the best stern face ever. She is very kind, but she does have definite ideas about how sand sprites should behave and she knows every single Rule in *The Sands of Time*.'

'Is she still unhappy about you dancing?' Shell asked.

'She'll always think it is the cause of misery and heartbreak, but she still makes me the most wonderful dancing clothes and gives me advice on how to improve my dancing. This time she made me a beautiful shrug to wear.'

'Sand sprites are complex creatures!' Shell looked serious as they continued their tour of the school.

They walked down the stairs and peeped into Miss Youngsand Jnr's science lab. It was all shiny and bright with rows of test tubes containing samples of sand from all over the world. The walls were covered with complicated charts and sprawling diagrams.

They crept down the long corridor and tiptoed past Madame Rosa's office. Cassie blushed as she recalled breaking into it the previous term when she was searching for information about her mother.

'It is good to know that, apart from the Secrets Cupboard, everything is exactly as we left it,' Cassie said.

'Except this,' Shell replied, as she and Cassie came to a freshly painted door at the far end of the corridor. They both looked at each other. The door had not been there the previous term.

Chapter Three

Beware of mirages in the desert.
Just because you want to see something
does not mean it is there.'
The Sands of Time

'It wouldn't do any harm to take a little peek inside, would it?' Shell's fingers twitched towards the handle.

Cassie frowned and stepped back. 'I don't want to get into trouble on the first day back.'

'This is absolutely the best time to get into trouble!' Shell quipped as she began to turn the handle. 'You tend to be let off precisely because it is the first day.'

Cassie felt the same prickle on the back of her neck as she had previously, but just as she was turning round to see who was behind her, someone called out to them brightly. 'There you are! I've been looking for you everywhere.'

Shell's hand moved away from the handle as if she had touched an electric eel. 'Don't do that ever again, Ella! My legs have turned to mush!'

'I didn't mean to scare you,' Ella apologised.

'We were just going to take a peek at what was behind that door,' Cassie explained. 'It wasn't there last term and we were curious.'

'If there are any adventures to be found, you won't be far away,' Ella said, glancing up admiringly at her two older friends.

Cassie shook her head and tried to look determined. 'This term I am only going to concentrate on dancing. That's all.'

'Then you won't be interested in the new music room,' Ella said, nodding towards the new door.

Shell waggled a finger at Ella. 'How come you always seem to know everything that is going on before anyone else?'

Ella beamed. 'I just keep my eyes and ears open, while trying to look like I'm not really listening. Thassalinus has been complaining about all the extra work he had creating a new room, and then I heard Madame Rosa say something about the new music room to Miss Youngsand Snr when I was unpacking my bag this afternoon.'

Shell whistled. 'Gentianella, you'd make a great spy.'

Ella grinned. 'Oh, thanks. Now, before we do anything else, I have to show you how to do a Sandringham Squeeze.'

'What's that?' Cassie and Shell both asked.

'My mother taught it to me over the holidays. She has started telling me about all the things she did when she was a trainee sand dancer, just before the school was closed down. To do the Squeeze you have to stand in a circle, cross your arms and hold hands, saying,

'Sandringham Squeeze, Sandringham Squeeze
Loyal and true till the oceans freeze.
Follow the dance steps from seven to one
You may take a little rest
After a Dune Arabesque
And take a lot of pride
In doing the perfect Sand Glide.
There's so much we can achieve
Sand dancing together
Floating along on a light sea breeze
You'll always find a friend
With a Sandringham Squeeze.'

'Then you pass a Squeeze around the circle and back again,' Ella explained.

'Bit quick as there are only three of us Squeezing,' Shell said, laughing. 'I'd like to see the whole school doing the Sandringham Squeeze. That would be something.'

The delicious smell of dinner wafted into the corridor, reminding the three sprites that it was time to make their way back to the dining hall.

'What do we need a music room for?' Cassie asked suddenly.

'I'm no expert but —' Shell began.

'A sand sprite can make one too many wisecracks, so please do not say anything about it being a room for music,' Cassie said. Then she turned to Ella. 'I'll ask someone sensible. What else do you know about the music room?'

Ella shook her head. 'That was all that I could pick up for now, but if I hear anything I'll let you know.' Her stomach rumbled. 'Hmm, something does smell good. It's like my nose has given my tummy permission to be hungry and I suddenly feel ravenous. Hope it's something filling.' Ella licked her lips.

'It is a sea cucumber stew,' Shell said.

'With a hint of wild thyme,' Cassie added as they entered the room.

'You are not the only one who has been doing some detective work today,' Shell told Ella as they took their places at one of the long wooden tables. 'Here come the teachers.'

The sand dancers all stood, as Madame Rosa, the principal, and the rest of the teachers came in and walked slowly towards their places at the top table. Mrs Sandskrit looked larger than ever in a new dress of bright purple with a long train decorated in tiny sea shells, and a long flowing turban on her head. Her sharp, bright eyes took in all the sprites.

28

Tall Miss Youngsand Jnr peered out at everyone from behind her glasses and smiled nervously, while her smaller but older twin (this fact was very important to Miss Youngsand Snr) checked everyone over and corrected one sand sprite's hair, which was too unruly, and another's posture. When she saw Shell's hair she did a double take and frowned.

'Sandrine does her hair like this at the moment,' Shell told her quickly, and nothing more was said about it.

Madame Rosa lifted one of her arms up with her usual multitude of bracelets jangling, signalling for everyone to sit down. Her violet-coloured eyes twinkled as she looked around the room and, in a warm clear voice, addressed the school.

'Welcome back to the Spring Term at the Sandringham Dance School. What a pleasure to see all of your eager faces at the start of this new term. Last term we were all settling in and getting the dance school up and running again after its long closure since the Night of the Great Sandstorm. I was so proud of the way you began your first steps on the journey to become sand dancers. We still have a lot of ground to make up, but I believe we are on our way to restoring the reputation of the sand dancers as a force for good and for nature. Now, let us eat. It is important that you all keep your strength up.'

Steaming bowls of sea cucumber stew and plates of samphire buns were passed around and everyone started to help themselves. Cassie tried to nibble politely on her bun, but her hunger got the better of her and she swallowed it down in two bites. Then she burped, earning a glare from Calluna who was sitting at the table opposite.

By the time the plates had been cleared away, all the sprites were feeling full, and Madame Rosa stood up to address them again.

'Now you have eaten it is time to give you some practical details for this term. You will all be issued with warm cloaks to wear to keep out the chill of the winter months. There will be extra science classes and nature walks led by Miss Youngsand Jnr. It is very important for a sand dancer to understand as much as she can about the flora and fauna of the dunes. A sand dancer must always try to be in perfect harmony with her surroundings. When she is, then she has a better chance of interpreting the dune dances correctly.'

Ella nudged Cassie. 'That must mean we are going to learn some secret dune dances!'

'I have also prepared some new experiments for us to try this term,' Miss Youngsand Jnr said shyly, and peeped at the sprites through her thick glasses.

All the sprites clapped and cheered, making Miss Youngsand Jnr blush even more and her twin sister, Miss Youngsand Snr, pursed her lips and snapped, 'Shhhh, sand sprites. Please, act with decorum!'

Madame Rosa raised a hand and the hall fell silent as she said in her soft voice, 'There will also be another additional lesson – slightly unusual perhaps.' Madame Rosa smiled at Mrs Sandskrit, who looked disapproving, but nodded graciously back.

Ella mouthed the word 'music' at Shell and Cassie, who tried not to laugh.

Madame Rosa continued. 'It is important to move with the times and not be afraid to try out new things. So this term we are introducing music lessons with a new guest teacher from a faraway dune. I believe that it is important for us to develop our musicality, if we are to really make the dunes sing. It is also important that we start to reach out and join up with our sister sprites from the many dunes of the world. We have been isolated for too long and are in danger of losing touch. Over the holidays, I was contacted by an old friend with whom I danced many moons ago. She had heard good reports about a certain music teacher, and so we have engaged her for a term's trial. This teacher is bringing her crystallophone with her. She is due to arrive tomorrow. I am sure you will all make her welcome.'

Even though it was against the Rules, the sand sprites couldn't help but begin to whisper about this.

A young sprite called Verbena raised her arm and curtseyed. 'Please, Madame Rosa, what is a crystallophone?'

Miss Youngsand Jnr stood up and replied, 'A crystallophone is a musical instrument made from glass. It's a glass harmonica which uses water in bowls to create a range of beautiful, inspirational sounds and there are also noises to be made from striking rows of glass. They are quite rare, and it is really exciting to have an opportunity to hear one.'

Madame Rosa clapped her hands, and the whispering subsided. 'I have spoken enough, so I will hand over to Mrs Sandskrit to tell you the most exciting news of all.'

The room fell quiet as Mrs Sandskrit took centre stage. No one dared talk while she was speaking. She scanned the room, frowned at a sand sprite who was fiddling with her braids and began. 'I am sure, like me, you are looking forward to continuing your training. Nothing worthwhile is ever achieved without a lot of hard work. Those of you who have spent time during your break sifting sand will know that. Sand dancers are the lucky ones, but we too have responsibilities always to do our best.'

Shell groaned. 'The Sand Dragon always takes the fun out of everything.'

Calluna shot her a warning look and hissed, 'Shh.'

Mrs Sandskrit dropped her voice and continued. 'Sometimes an unexpected opportunity comes along that we must take. Miss Youngsand Jnr has been doing some calculations.'

Miss Youngsand Jnr stepped forward once more. 'Most seasons only have three full moons, but very rarely a season will have one extra full moon. This spring, in two months' time, there will be a fourth full moon, known as a blue moon, which means only one thing . . .' She blinked excitedly.

To everyone's surprise, it was Calluna who blurted out, 'A Blue Moon Ballet! It means there's going to be a Blue Moon Ballet!' Then she clamped her hand to her mouth, blushed deeply and tried to shrink down in her chair.

'A Blue Moon Ballet, indeed. Calluna is right,' Madame Rosa said, smiling. 'This ballet is one of our secret dune dances. We would not usually teach you this dance just yet, but as nature has intervened and sent us a blue moon we must act accordingly. It will not be easy, but if we can perform it at all well it will help to maintain the health and harmony of our beloved sand dunes.'

'I've heard it is a really hard ballet to perform with lots of tricky moves,' Ella pondered aloud.

Shell nodded. 'Because a blue moon so rarely occurs, it is not performed often.'

'And now *we* have a chance to perform in it,' Cassie whispered excitedly. Then another thought struck her. 'If we perform the ballet, we are actually helping to pre-serve the dunes.' She looked around the room which was bubbling with excitement and laughter, and won-dered how the dancers would react if they knew that the life of the dunes and all the plants and creatures who lived there depended so much on them. She imagined the pressure and panic if they knew just how serious the situation was – that the dunes were dying.

'It is a very complicated ballet with some challenging sequencing, including a breathtaking solo moon dance,'

Mrs Sandskrit continued.

'No one will be ready to perform that,' Madame Rosa said. 'But we shall be looking carefully and selecting those dancers who demonstrate the most affinity with the moon to perform in some of the other sequences. Those selected dancers will have the honour of being loaned a copy of the precious Blue Moon booklet, revealing the whole dance sequence as it is performed on the night.'

Madame Rosa paused. 'There is one final detail. Nearer the time, we must all be prepared to become nocturnal. Because the ballet will be performed at night by the light of the moon, we must begin to rehearse in the evening.'

'How thrilling! I love staying up late,' Ella said.

'Some of us are good at that already.' Shell winked at Cassie. 'It must be time for a moonlight picnic soon.'

'No,' Ella laughed, 'this term the daring thing to do will be to have a sunshine picnic when everyone is asleep! Don't you agree, Cassie?'

But Cassie was not listening. Her tummy tingled and her heart felt excited and nervous. All she could think about was the Blue Moon Ballet. Would she be able to dance in harmony with the moon and be chosen to become one of the selected dancers? That would surely make her mother proud.

Chapter Four

'Dance, dance, to the music of the sands of time.'
The Sands of Time

Mrs Sandskrit looked very serious as she sailed into the practice studio the next morning. Her flowing ink-blue dress billowed around her large round body and the silvery grey turban made her look even taller than she was. There was a large moonstone and crystal brooch pinned to the centre of the turban that shimmered in the light. The moment she was inside the room, she clapped her hands and signalled for the sprites to find a space and, with a crisp voice she said, 'Let us start with a recap of the seven basic dance steps. Step one – the Sand Stretch. Now let's put some elasticity in those legs . . .'

All the sand sprites got into position and began to repeat the stretch in time with each other, over and over again, with Mrs Sandskrit correcting the stance of a sprite here, and the arms of a sprite there. She called out the names of the seven basic dance steps in turn and everyone tried to do their best to perform each to Mrs Sandskrit's satisfaction.

Although Cassie had been practising over the holidays, it was hard work and soon tiny beads of sweat ran down her face. During the Sand Glide, she particularly struggled to coordinate her arms and legs, and couldn't stop a smile forming when she remembered how it had felt when she had tied dusters to her feet and polished the tables in the dining hall to get the movement right.

'Cassandra Marramgrass! Training to be a sand dancer is not supposed to be fun!' Mrs Sandskrit glared at her. 'If you have the energy to grin, then you are not concentrating hard enough. Exercise class is not a walk on the beach!'

'Sorry, Mrs Sandskrit,' Cassie murmured and she focused even harder.

Everyone felt tired and hot after the class.

'Phew! That was tough.' Shell fanned her pink face with one of her slippers as they changed out of their practice clothes.

Ella tied her hair back into a tidy bun. 'Mrs Sandskrit is always strict and works us hard, but today it felt different. It was as if she was taking something out on us.'

'It doesn't seem fair that we should have even more work to do in each lesson just because the music class takes the place of an exercise class,' Cassie grumbled.

'It's hard enough knowing that we have the Blue Moon Ballet to perform at the end of term,' Shell added, 'without the idea of music lessons putting the Sand Dragon in a grump.'

'I am not going to let anything spoil the excitement of the Blue Moon Ballet.' Ella flicked the ribbon of her dancing slipper at Shell.

Calluna said, 'It would be good to show the world that the sand dancers are back on form. Blue Moon Ballet performances are legendary. If the sequences are correctly performed the dunes will sing out. Sandrine would be so proud of us and even the Prince of Tides might be impressed when he hears about it.'

'For once, Calluna, I totally agree with you!' Shell nodded at Calluna. 'It would be great to remind the Prince of Tides just how important and talented sand dancers really are.'

Shell's eyes flashed and her fingers trembled as she put her practice clothes away. 'I saw the Prince of Tides at the palace during the holidays. I was putting the teacups in Sandrine's Official Tea Service away in their special display cabinet when I overheard a conversation between Sandrine and him and I wasn't impressed with his attitude. It was like he felt that his ability to control the tides was much more important than Sandrine's ability to control the dunes, that he was more important than us ordinary sand sprites. There was something about him that reminded me of a doodlebug. Just like those creatures that burrow in the sand, I imagined him lying in wait to grab you unexpectedly,' Shell said grimly.

'But everyone says how handsome and striking he is,' Ella said.

Shell tapped her nose. 'It's all camouflage. Think doodlebug.'

'I'd rather not think about being squashed by a large bug,' Ella said, squirming.

'You think doodlebugs are scary, but think what they eventually turn into – great big scary sand lions! They can swallow up sand sprites!' Shell exclaimed in a loud voice.

'Has the new music teacher arrived yet?' Cassie said, changing the subject.

Ella shook her head. 'No one has seen her yet, but I do know her name – it's Miss Bluegrass.'

'That's an unusual name. I've never heard of a blue grass growing in the dunes,' Cassie said. 'Are you sure you've got the name right?'

'I saw Thassalinus bringing in a large wooden crate with the word *Bluegrass* written on it,' Ella explained.

'My little spy!' Shell winked. 'Nothing escapes you.'

'We will have to wait for our first lesson to find out for certain.' Calluna spoke in a bossy voice and glared at everyone. 'And we should be getting changed in silence.'

After lunch, Shell pulled Cassie to one side. 'Let's go for

a quick stroll on the beach. I need some fresh air.'

'Are you sure we have time?' Cassie asked. She was still a bit shaken by Mrs Sandskrit's comments about her dancing and wanted some time alone to think about it.

'We've got the rest of lunch break – and a walk will do us good. I got too wound up talking about the Prince of Tides.'

'That's the first time I've ever seen you agree with Calluna.' Cassie laughed, but Shell looked worried as they went outside.

'I can't put it exactly into words but there is something about the Prince that I don't trust. When he visited us at the palace he was polite, but all the same I felt that he was sizing us up and coming to the conclusion that we are weak and pathetic. He kept commenting on the state of the dunes, saying that if Sandrine had any real power they would be flourishing, like his sea kingdom. He was very keen to know how much power we still had over nature.'

'We have rebuilt the dunes after the Great Sandstorm and we are starting to dance again, which will help to maintain them,' Cassie said proudly.

'He probably doesn't like the idea of us getting stronger while he has to struggle all the time to control the tides and the seas,' Shell replied.

'How did Sandrine deal with him?' Cassie asked.

'With perfect manners, but I could see that she was concerned about his constant probing. So were all the Senior Sand Sprites at the palace. He was very interested in the fact that the dance school had reopened, and the power that our dancing has to protect the dunes. In fact, he seemed distinctly too interested.'

'But surely he has to do what Sandrine commands?' Cassie replied.

'He hates her being more powerful. They can't force each other to do anything, so they have to get on. The Prince of Tides controls the surf boys, but the sand farers are always loyal to Sandrine.' Shell chewed anxiously on her bottom lip.

'Don't worry. Sandrine will find a way to deal with him and my mother will be back soon with all the dune dances, which will gives us loads more power and show him a thing or two!' Cassie tried to reassure her friend, but she really wished that Lexie were here – she always had a calming influence.

'I'm also surprised that there was no talk of a Blue Moon Ballet at the palace,' Shell said.

'Maybe Miss Youngsand Jnr has only just done the right astronomical calculations,' Cassie suggested.

'Or maybe Sandrine wanted to keep the news quiet. She's always edgy when the Prince of Tides is around. They have different domains to control, but like the sand and sea, their kingdoms overlap and they are always disagreeing about the best ways to rule the sand sprites. He always seems to know what is happening on the dunes without her telling him. He knew exactly when Silica City had been rebuilt and all about the dance school.'

'Surf boys are constantly moving around, racing their sand surfers, sand boarding or delivering messages. They are bound to find things out.' Cassie thought about Rubus.

Shell took a deep breath. 'I shouldn't be telling you this but . . . we also think he has a lot of spies.'

'Surely he doesn't mean us any harm?'

Shell didn't reply for a long time before saying, 'I hope not. I don't completely trust him. I certainly wouldn't want him finding out too much about our secret dune dances.'

They strolled past the swimming pool and down to the edge of the dune.

Shell continued. 'I nearly gave myself away to Ella when I was talking about the Prince of Tides.'

She leaned back on the side of a rock and let out a long sigh of frustration.

Cassie joined her, saying, 'You could make life easier for yourself and let everybody know who you really are.'

Shell shook her head and her blue eyes flashed. 'No way. This is my one chance to show everyone what I can achieve without any special treatment or privileges. I would rather be known as Shell, the servant sprite who was a good enough dancer to win a place at Sandringham on her own merits.'

Cassie handed her a samphire bun that she'd smuggled out of lunch. 'Dancing makes me so hungry all the time.'

They munched in silence for a while, looking out to sea.

'Aren't these buns Rubus's favourite?' Shell asked as she took a large bite.

'Rubus eats anything he can get his hands on, but he likes samphire buns and seaweed pasties best of all,' Cassie said between mouthfuls.

'Have you heard from him?' Shell asked.

'He doesn't write so well and besides he might not be able to. He's on a secret mission, after all.' Cassie rolled her eyes and smiled. 'He will be impossible when he does get back. I'll have to listen to all his endless sand-farer tales . . . But at least his return will mean that my mother is back too – I hope.'

'That will be wonderful for you – and for all the sand dancers. It will be amazing to have our prima dune dancer here again! Think of the things she will be able to show us! We'll be ten times more powerful when she comes back,' Shell said.

Cassie smoothed a patch of sand. 'Let's go over the seven basic dance steps before we leave. Then I won't feel so guilty for breaking the Rules and leaving the school without permission.'

She looked out to sea. Talking about Rubus had made Cassie feel grumpled. They had been friends since they were sand babies and he always knew how she was feeling and cheered her up if she was upset or miserable.

Shell nudged her arm. 'Come on, I thought we were supposed to be dancing and not daydreaming.'

Without another word, Cassie and Shell stood tall

and began to move through the seven dance steps, bending and flexing gracefully and seamlessly from one to the next. At first they were slightly out of step, but as they began to concentrate their moves began to flow together.

When they were doing the Dart and Turn for the second time, Cassie felt the now familiar prickle on the back of her neck, and her eyes were drawn to a flash of green in the tufts of grass. To start with, she thought it was a piece of shiny glass, but when she looked again she saw a twinkling pair of eyes watching them intently.

Shell spotted them at the same time, froze mid-turn and shouted, 'What do you think you are doing?' She raced towards the tuft of grass, and a surf boy slowly rose up from between the blades.

Cassie strode after her. 'You're not supposed to be here – you'll get into big trouble.'

The surf boy bowed in greeting. He was very tall with long legs, a sturdy body and a mass of long dark ringlets. In true surf boy fashion, he wasn't wearing a shirt, but he was wearing some sort of harness around his shoulders.

He smiled at them as he straightened up. He smelled of wet sand mingled with wild thyme. It was a familiar smell to Cassie, but she couldn't think why.

'You're sand dancers, aren't you? I'm thrilled to meet you.'

'And you are . . .?' Shell asked in a haughty voice.

'I am Lysander,' he replied. 'I am sorry to have startled

you. Your dancing was amazing. This move was amazing.'

He sprang forward and raised his leg up behind him in a near perfect Dune Arabesque.

'Where did you learn to do that?' Cassie whistled. It had taken her weeks to even begin to get that move right and she was still trying to perfect it.

'I just watched you doing it,' he said simply, turning towards them with a friendly grin. 'I didn't catch your names.'

Shell drew herself up into a dignified sand dancer pose and said in her best snooty voice, 'We did not choose to give you that information without a formal introduction. Everyone knows that a sand dancer must behave with decorum at all times.'

Cassie tried to smother her giggles. Her friend was always breaking that Rule herself. When Shell turned and glared at her she pretended she was coughing.

'How did you come to be in Dreamy Dune?' Cassie asked. 'It's a hard place to get to.' She looked around for a sand board or sand sailing ship, the usual forms of transport for surf boys. There was none to be seen.

Lysander repositioned himself into a copy of Shell's stance and replied in a perfect imitation of her voice. 'What if I choose not to tell you?'

They all laughed, and the tension was broken.

'I *will* choose to tell you, though,' continued Lysander. 'Believe it or not, I hitched a lift on a Blown By The Wind jellyfish. Jellycoptering is my favourite form of transport. In fact, it took two jellies, one for me and one for my belongings.' He glanced back at the empty beach. 'The other one must be running late – there were some strong currents nearby.'

'Jellycoptering? I've never heard of it!' Cassie spluttered.

Lysander shrugged his shoulders, which made his dark ringlets shake as he replied slowly and carefully. 'I invented it. You have to find a cooperative jellyfish. Blown By The Wind jellyfish are the best, because they have a float. It is full of gas, which can be a bit smelly, but it can fill the sail you need to bring along. It's a stinky but exhilarating experience.'

'What does the Prince of Tides say about it? Doesn't sound like something he'd approve of one of his surf boys doing.' Shell tried to sound casual, but Cassie could hear that she was rattled by Lysander's presence.

Lysander waved his hand dismissively. 'He is far too busy to bother about what a cheeky surf boy like me is getting up to. Besides, he likes us to be a bit wild and show some spirit. It is a private arrangement between me and the jellyfish.'

'And what exactly are you doing over this way?' Shell arched an eyebrow.

Lysander spun round and gave a perfect Dart and Turn. 'Just travelling . . . But please, don't let me stop you dancing – if you don't mind an audience.' He sat himself back down in the sea grass.

'You really like dancing?' Cassie asked.

'He's a surf boy, of course he doesn't like dancing. He is just winding us up,' Shell said.

Lysander frowned at them. 'Even though you don't appear to trust me, I will trust you enough to let you in on a secret. I shall tell you about the best moment in my entire life.'

They both looked at him, intrigued, but Shell quickly replied, 'Who says we'd be interested?'

He paused and then got up to leave.

'Oh, well, you can tell us if you must!' wailed Shell.

Lysander instantly sat down again. When he spoke, it was with a quiet excitement. 'When I was a little sand boy, I saw Marina Marramgrass dance.'

Cassie gasped. 'What! You – you couldn't have . . .' Her heart flip-flopped in her stomach.

Lysander stared out to sea with a dreamy expression as he went on. 'Believe what you will, but one night, many moons ago, Marina Marramgrass paid a visit to my dune. It is far away from here. She stayed for three days. Most of the time she was in meetings with the elders, but on the last night she put on a performance for everyone in the market place.' Lysander's eyes shone. 'It was the most beautiful thing that I've ever seen. The way that she danced was so much finer than the dune dancers I had seen performing in our area. The crowd was silent and after her dance the dunes rang out for a few seconds. It was as if she was flying when she moved her legs like . . . like . . . oh, like this.'

He stood up, jumped and tried to cross his legs quickly and in fast repetition. 'I love to try and move as she did, and I've been trying to copy that move ever since. One day I will be able to do that magical step. I will!' His green eyes shone with passion and determination.

'That move is called the Triple Silica Jump and only the finest prima dune dancers can perform it,' Cassie said in a proud voice.

'A Triple Silica Jump,' Lysander said, enjoying the words on his tongue like a delicious flavour. 'I have always longed to know what that move was called. Thank you so much for telling me.' He smiled at Cassie.

'It is a truly powerful dance step,' she said as her cheeks flushed pink.

'Can you do one for me? I would love to learn how to do it. It must be like flying – without the aid of a jellyfish!'

'You have to train for ages and ages to get it right. Every dancer begins by practising the seven basic dance steps and if they are good enough, they can then become part of the performing dune dancers, and learn the secret dune dances,' Cassie explained.

'Sounds wonderful. How do the secret dune dances go? Can you do any of them?' Lysander's face lit up as he fired eager questions at them.

'Why are you so interested?' Shell's voice was harsh, and her eyes narrowed with suspicion.

Lysander looked back at her, his green eyes flashing once more. 'As a traveller, I am interested in the customs

47

of all the places I visit. Now, mysterious and nameless sand dancers, I must be on my way. But first I have to ask a favour of you. Can you show me the way to Silica City?'

Cassie pointed in one direction at the same moment that Shell pointed in another.

Lysander's eyes twinkled. 'I wonder whose sense of direction I am going to put my trust in?' He bowed low. 'I am sure we will meet again.'

Like quicksilver, he raced down to the shore making a strange whistling sound and dived into the sea.

Shell and Cassie watched him leave. He kept turning around and waving at them until he was completely out of view.

'And I thought this term was going to be pleasantly dull with nothing but dancing and my friends to concentrate on,' said Shell grumpily. 'First we find out that Lexie won't be back right away and that we are having music lessons. Then we find out about the Blue Moon Ballet. And to top it all, a mysterious surf boy lands in our midst asking too many questions for my liking. Like he would really be interested in dancing!'

'He seemed so keen when he spoke about Marina dancing,' said Cassie dreamily.

'Doodlebug,' replied Shell. 'Grr. I think I will have to do three Frustration Flips to recover!' She spun round and turned three cartwheels on the sand, Cassie joining in with her.

When they finally collapsed in a heap, Cassie said,

'Rubus was just the same, though. He liked to travel to different places too. Travelling is just something surf boys get to do. Lysander is probably just curious about dancing since it's something surf boys don't do, but he certainly has a natural talent for it.'

Shell was silent for a while. 'I don't know what to think. We are supposed to keep our dance training secret and only share it with other sand dancers. That way we can guard the mystery of the dance steps. The dances have to be performed in a certain way to maintain their power. If Lysander were serious about dancing, and I don't believe for one second that he is, then he would have to learn the right combinations – and no one will teach him that!'

'Do you think we should tell anyone else about Lysander?' Cassie asked.

Shell shook her head. 'That would only make things harder for us, if we have said too much. Until we have some proof that he isn't just passing by like he said, we'd better keep quiet or we'll have a much harder time sneaking out in the future!'

Chapter Five

*'Quicksand and firmsand look the same
so know the ground well before you tread on it.'
The Sands of Time*

Cassie and Shell were just back in time for their afternoon sewing class with Miss Youngsand Snr. She fixed them with a stern look as they entered the room. 'Thank you so much for gracing us with your presence,' she harrumphed at them, as they took their places around the large round table covered with neat piles of material and tight skeins of soft-coloured threads. The moment they sat down she tapped the table. 'Sand sprites, take up your handkerchiefs and start tacking.'

The class gathered up their needles and began. Before long, there was a steady movement of hands rising and falling around the table.

Miss Youngsand Snr watched them closely as they

worked in silence, making occasional comments like, 'Tension, too much tension,' or 'Fingers as light as a soft summer sea breeze!'

Cassie found it easy to let her hands sew while her mind drifted, and she was still thinking about her encounter with Lysander. Now that she had recovered from the shock of hearing that he had seen her mother dance, so many questions jumped into her head that she should have asked him. What had her mother looked like? Had she said anything about coming home? Did she say anything about her daughter? All these questions buzzed around in her head like angry sand flies. Why hadn't she thought to ask them at the time?

There was also something strange about that surf boy. His dancing was too good, for one thing. Could he really have just picked it up from watching them on the beach? If that was the case then he had an incredible gift. It was clear Shell didn't trust him. Cassie found herself wishing again that Lexie was there. Or Rubus – he would have worked out if Lysander was really up to something. Cassie smiled to herself. Rubus would love to have a ride on a jellyfish. He would probably dare her to have a go too, and then they could race on them, and Cassie would try her best to beat him. Sensible Lexie would try equally hard to keep Cassie on the beach, before cheering her on.

A lump welled up in Cassie's throat as she realised just how much she missed having Rubus and Lexie around her.

I must not allow myself to become distracted like I did last term, or my dancing will suffer. Cassie blinked away some tears and looked down at her handkerchief. Her stitches were all uneven. Slowly and carefully she began to unpick them, and then she started all over again.

Fifteen minutes later, Miss Youngsand Snr told the class to finish off the stitch they were working on and fold their handkerchiefs neatly away. 'Sewing is a bit like dancing. I always like to start my sewing classes with some good honest plain stitches to get your fingers warmed up. This term you will all be embroidering a small blue moon on the side of your bags to show that you have performed the ballet.' She held up a drawing of the outline of an inky moon reflecting on the sea with dunes in the foreground, and smiled one of her rare smiles. 'I designed the pattern myself from my memory of the last time a Blue Moon Ballet was performed.'

'Please could you tell us about it?' a brave sprite asked.

All the class joined in. 'Yes, please tell us.'

Miss Youngsand Snr put down her needle and the class held its breath, waiting to be told off for being impertinent. But instead, she sighed and said, 'Oh my, it was wonderful. The school was almost twice the size then. We built a fine stage on the edge of the dune and lots of important sprites were invited. The Prince of Tides sent us a beautiful selection of shells to decorate the stage – not the current prince, but the one before, who was Sandrine's father. What a gracious sprite he was! He kept surf boys in their proper place. He controlled the tides beautifully and rhythmically and knew when to use force and when to hold back. Controlling the tides is like sand dancing – you have to have a talent and a feel for it. One false step and things can easily spiral out of control.'

'Could our Prince of Tides have lost control and caused a sandstorm?' Cassie asked, thinking out loud.

Mrs Youngsand Snr replied in a sharp tone, 'No one knows the exact cause of the Great Sandstorm, Cassie. And it is not wise to speculate or lay blame. The storm was one of those unexplainable mysteries of nature that occur from time to time.

'Now, we must all concentrate our energy on the business in hand – the preparation and performance of the Blue Moon Ballet. It is one of the most atmospheric ballets that we perform. It is also one of the saddest. The ballet is all about looking back and regretting and wishing for a better life ahead. There is an amazing solo spot for the prima dune dancer to perform, where she dances with the moon. It is such a strong and beautiful dance that the dunes vibrate with the memory of what they have lost, and we are left with a stronger resolve to preserve what we have.'

'Are you sure no one is able to perform the solo?' Calluna asked hopefully. She was the senior sand dancer and was expected to take a lead in many things.

Miss Youngsand Snr shook her head. 'I don't think

anyone is ready yet. Not even our most promising student, Alexsandra Seacouch, could attempt it yet. Of course, she is not here at present.'

'Good, it will give the rest of us a chance to show what we can do,' Calluna said quietly, and a lot of the sprites around the table muttered in agreement.

Miss Youngsand Snr glared at them. 'There has been enough talking and time wasting. We will continue the lesson in silence. You can chalk the design on to your bags and begin embroidering an outline. Shell, I can see that you will have to stay behind for some extra tuition before you can begin yours.'

Cassie had felt a jolt when she heard Lexie's name. Lexie was missing out on all the excitement of the Blue Moon Ballet. If she were there, she would have been practising frantically and wishing desperately that she would be selected for the special group. Lexie was probably the only person in the school who did not realise that she was one of its finest dancers. Lexie's mother, Viola Seacouch, had trained as a dancer before the school was closed down. She now sold sea cakes to make a living. She was very proud of Lexie, and Cassie hoped that one day her mother would be just as proud of her.

Then a colder thought crept into her brain. As Lexie was not back yet, *she* might have more of a chance of being selected for the special group dance. Wasn't Mrs Sandskrit always telling them that sand dancers had to be ruthless when it came to winning parts? Perhaps she shouldn't be feeling so sorry for Lexie . . .

At the end of the lesson, Cassie bumped into Thassalinus, who was sweeping the corridor. He beckoned her over. 'I am going to visit Viola Seacouch to collect a food order for the school in a moment. I could deliver a note to young Lexie, if you like. I know how you sprites pine for your friends.'

'Oh, thank you! That would be fantastic! You must have been reading my mind!'

She hugged Thassalinus, who became all gruff and replied sharply, 'I'm leaving in twenty minutes, so you'd better hurry up and write it. As if I'd have the time or the inclination to try and read a sand dancer's mind. Huh.'

Cassie raced to her room, found a scrap of paper, and wrote quickly.

Dear Lexie,

I am scribbling you this note so Thassalinus can deliver it. I was sooo surprised to hear from Ella about your leg being so bad. Thought you might have dropped me a line. Please hurry up and get well, because Sandringham is strange without having you to talk to. We bumped into a surf boy on the beach. He was asking lots of questions about dancing. Shell is as crazy as ever. She has the most amazing hairstyle at the moment. It's like she has two giant samphire buns plastered to her head. The big news at school is that we —

Cassie paused. She was going to tell Lexie all about the

Blue Moon Ballet, but what if Lexie rushed back and got one of the special parts that could have gone to her? She sighed and finished off the sentence.

— are going to have music lessons. No idea what they will be like or who the new teacher is, only that she is called Miss Bluegrass and she plays a crystallophone.

Then she changed her mind again. It seemed strange not to tell Lexie when it was such a big part of their lives, so she added,

Best of all we are going to perform the Blue Moon Ballet. Don't know much about it yet, apart from it is a dreamy but hard ballet to perform.

There was no more space to write anything else and Thassalinus was waiting for the letter, so there was only time to scribble her name at the bottom. Cassie would have to tell her more about the Blue Moon Ballet, and whether she had a part in it or not, in the next letter. She might also have some more news about the mysterious Lysander.

As she watched Thassalinus walk off, she couldn't help but hope a little that Lexie would not come back too soon. She needed to improve her dancing, get chosen for the select dance group and impress her mother.

Chapter Six

'Wishing wells do not quench your thirst.'
The Sands of Time

The next morning was their first interpretation class with Madame Rosa. The sprites made their way excitedly past the swimming pool and down the stone steps that led to the shell grotto. This was Madame Rosa's favourite room for teaching in – she said that it had a very special atmosphere that helped with finding the right inspiration to dance.

Madame Rosa was standing next to the large fountain and shell sculpture that stood in the middle of the room. She was wearing a simple green dress, but her arms, as always, were covered with lots of glass bracelets. The colours of her bracelets were all greens and blues that day, and they jangled and reflected rays of light as she moved.

'Today's class begins with a story,' she said, as the

sand sprites sat down on the low wall surrounding the green fountain. 'There are many stories and legends associated with the blue moon. Today I am going to tell you one story that is as old as *The Sands of Time*.

'Long, long ago, when the Earth was but a few grains of sand and the dunes were just beginning to form, there was no dancing and all the sand sprites – male and female – lived together in harmony with all the other creatures of the Earth. The planet was not formed as it is now. Legend tells that the sun and the moon shared the sky. They would shine together and it was light all the time.

'One day an inquisitive young sand sprite looked up at the sky and exclaimed to her mother, "Look at the reflection of the sun."

'Her mother laughed. "That is not the sun's reflection. That is the moon."

'"But it is so pale. There is no point to it," the young sand sprite complained. "What a waste of light."'

Madame Rosa stood up and recreated that part of the story as a series of dance moves. At first her body turned into a young giggling sand sprite pointing at the moon, and then it turned into a sparkling sun and moon dance step.

She stopped and continued speaking in a sad, low tone.

'"Shh," her mother said. "Speak softly for you do not want to upset the moon."

'But the moon had heard and she was very sad. "I am no use. No one can really see me. What use am I?"

'And so she went away and hid herself inside a very dark cloud. She became so sad that her skin turned a pale blue.

'Her sister, the sun, tried to bring her round. "Of course you are of use. You are my sister. I would be lost without you. I will stop shining so brightly for half of the time so that everyone can appreciate your delicate glow."

'The moon replied, "No, I do not want to succeed by your failure, my bright sister sun." And so the moon returned to her cold dark hiding place, leaving her sister to shine in the sky.

'But even the moon could not feel sorry for herself for ever. When her sister was taking a nap, she decided to come out and cast her pale silvery beams over the sky. It was fun to glide and send winking beams of light to play on the rivers and oceans. So she acted as a searchlight for lost creatures to find their way home.

'In the silence and the darkness, she was completely overcome by an irresistible urge to dance across the sky. And, as she did so, she felt something moving along beside her, in tune with her rhythm. When she turned around, she saw that she had pulled the ocean along with her. She felt powerful, but exhausted. "I may not be as bright as the sun, but I have a part to play. I can work when she is resting and I can command the tides.

Some creatures find the sun too bright, so I can provide a gentler glow for them. Here in the dark of night I can shine. Some plants and seeds may even prefer the moonlight to grow." '

Madame began to dance again. At first she became the pale sad moon in despair, but gradually she began to shine and she moved in a beautiful joyous dance. Her body was powerful and moved with ease. She danced in small delicate movements that flowed gracefully into one another and kept everyone enraptured.

When she had finished and got her breath back, she turned to the class and said, 'When you find your place in the world it is truly a beautiful moment.'

Cassie thought this was the most wonderful thing she had ever heard.

Madame Rosa walked around the fountain looking at each dancer in turn. 'Since we do not have a prima dune dancer, we are modifying the ballet. Five dancers will be chosen to dance a piece based on the sequences of the main solo. The part when the prima dune dancer usually dances with the Blue Moon will be replaced with melody and song.'

'Madame Rosa,' a young sand sprite asked, 'why don't *you* dance the solo?' and then she blushed.

Madame Rosa smiled. 'I only wish I could, but knowing the steps and being able to run a dancing school is a very different matter from having the talent to dance. Maybe a few years ago I would have attempted it, but not any more. I am too old. My time for performing has passed by, as it has for many other sand dancers. Closing the school for seven years has meant that we have lost a generation of dancers. Once time has slipped through your fingers you cannot get it back. And I'm afraid that no one here is quite ready yet. We will hold auditions for the principal dancers and they will have to work incredibly hard to recreate the Blue Moon magic instead.'

As she was leaving the grotto, Madame Rosa handed them all a sheet with some dance sequences on it.

'We will be working on these sequences in class to perform in the ballet itself. You will notice there is a space in the middle. The challenge for your audition will be for each of you to fill that space in your own unique way.'

At the end of the lesson no one wanted to leave. Everyone lingered around the fountain.

'*When you find your place in the world it is truly a beautiful moment,*' Cassie repeated out loud. 'I hope I can find my true place,' she whispered.

'Listening to the story and watching the dancing made me feel dreamy,' said Ella, dipping her hand into the fountain. 'Oh, I do hope I'll get picked to perform the main dance.'

All the sand dancers felt the same.

Chapter Seven

'What makes the dunes sing aloud?
Follow your heart and you may find out.'
The Sands of Time

Calluna sniffed and folded her arms. 'I don't see why we have to have music lessons. It has never been heard of before at Sandringham.'

'We are sand *dancers*, not sand *singers*,' another sprite said, joining in the grumbling.

'The time would be better spent preparing for the Blue Moon Ballet,' someone else added, and everyone muttered in agreement.

They were all standing outside the door to the music room. Cassie shivered as it was draughty in the corridor and she had been hot after Mrs Sandskrit's class. She wished she had brought her shrug along. It would've been perfect to drape around her bare shoulders to keep the cold out. Instead, she stamped her feet to keep warm and breathed deeply. As she sniffed, she became aware of a scent. There was that familiar whiff of wild thyme that she smelled on the first day when she had been convinced that someone was hiding in the corridor. She tried as discreetly as she could to sniff around to see if she could detect where it was coming from.

'Keep your distance from me if you are beginning a cold.' Calluna stepped back from Cassie.

'Madame Rosa thinks that music will help to develop our musicality and rhythm,' Shell said, continuing the debate.

'And music is to replace part of the prima dune dancer's solo, so it is important to the ballet,' Cassie added.

'I think someone should be given the opportunity to dance a solo, instead of having some music to replace it,' Calluna said sourly. 'Especially now Lexie Seacouch is not here to hog all the attention.'

Several sprites nodded.

'And I thought we were all trying to dance our best to help everything stay healthy and harmonious,' Shell said sarcastically.

'And what have you done to your hair, Ella?' Calluna demanded as the young sprite joined them.

Ella ignored her, looking at the closed door.

'Your hair. What have you done to your hair?' Calluna asked again in a louder voice.

Ella smiled. 'Thank you, I always try to be fair.'

Calluna lifted one of her braids and shouted in her ear, 'WHAT HAVE YOU DONE TO YOUR HAIR?'

'There's no need to shout. It is the latest fashion at the palace.' Ella patted the two enormous bun rings at either side of her head. They were about twice as thick as Shell's.

Calluna sighed. 'I expect you mean that spoiled brat Anagallis is wearing her hair like that.'

'Is she?' Ella asked Shell. 'You work at the palace. Did the spoiled brat insist on it?'

Shell winked at Cassie. 'Indeed. Anagallis is far too lazy to do her own hair. I had to arrange it for her every day. You'd be amazed at some of the things I found hidden inside her braids.'

'I wonder how she is getting on without you,' Ella continued. 'I always thought that once the dance school opened again she would want to join – and being Sandrine's daughter, she'd get a place automatically, without having to pass an audition like the rest of us.'

Calluna shook her head. 'Can you imagine how she would cope without getting her own way all the time? She wouldn't last five minutes here. She'd be screaming and running out of the door after one of Mrs Sandskrit's classes.'

'We're not all used to as strict an upbringing as you are,' Shell bristled back, in such a fierce way that Calluna blushed.

Everyone knew that Calluna's mother was very strict and placed lots of demands on her daughter. Cassie felt a bit sorry for her. It wasn't fair of Shell to bring that up. It wasn't Calluna's fault she'd upset her – she didn't know Shell was really Anagallis.

Lexie would have known what to say, and would have tried to be kind to Calluna. Cassie felt a pang of shame and wished she hadn't felt so jealous when she had written that note to her. She felt mean and low. Why couldn't she just be proud of her friend's talent and try to be as much like her as possible?

At that moment, the door sprang open and a loud voice boomed, 'What is this hullabaloo outside my door?'

There was silence. Everyone stared in amazement at the figure in the doorway. No one had seen a sand sprite like this before, let alone one that was a teacher at Sandringham Dance School. Cassie blinked and looked again, just in case her eyes were deceiving her. Standing in the doorway was a tiny sprite with bright yellow hair braided into a tall elaborate arrangement adorned with pearls, clips, chimes and bells. It seemed that her hair was almost the same size as her body.

Miss Bluegrass smiled and patted her head. 'So you like my hairdo. It's how we all wear our hair where I come from.'

She spoke with a twangy accent that Cassie had never heard. But before she could wonder any more about it,

Miss Bluegrass had pulled out a small crystal flute from her hairband and began to play brightly, waving the stick to indicate that the sprites were to come inside. Stunned, they all followed her into the long and narrow room that had recently been hollowed out of the dune to create the new music room.

The sprites gasped when the flute changed colour from clear crystal to blue to green, violet and red until Miss Bluegrass finished her tune.

'When I have completely unpacked, I'll have one of these flutes for each of you. They make handy hair clips too.' She gave it a final toot and popped it back into her hair. 'Welcome to your first official music class. Sand sprites, and sand dancers in particular, are by nature musical beings. You might not play instruments, but when you are dancing you respond to the rhythms and sounds of nature. There is music within you waiting to burst out. My job over the next few weeks will be to develop your musicality. So our musical journey of discovery begins today. Music is all around us and that is what I want you to work on today. I want you to find some sounds and respond to them.'

She shook her head, causing the chimes and bells to tinkle and ring. Someone laughed nervously. No one was quite sure what to do next, but Miss Bluegrass pounced on the sprite that laughed.

'Good to hear a noise coming from you at last. Are you sprites usually so quiet? Come on, gather round and tell me all your names.'

The sprites formed a circle and someone tried to suppress a nervous giggle. Mrs Sandskrit would've frowned at this, but Miss Bluegrass only grinned at them.

'The first thing I want you all to do is to shout your name at the top of your voice as loudly as you can. Let me demonstrate.' Miss Bluegrass picked two flutes out of her hair, placed one on either side of her mouth and sounded a loud, high note. Then she shouted at the top of her voice, 'TULAROSA BLUEGRASS!'

The high-pitched shout seemed to reverberate around the room and bounce off the walls and Miss Bluegrass laughed. 'Your turn now, sand dancers. Off you go, all together.' She blew on her flutes again to cue them.

The first attempt was a shy noise. She tooted a second time and the next one was a little louder. By the third attempt, the whole class was bellowing and shrieking out their names.

Miss Bluegrass waved her flute at them encouragingly and kept on nodding and saying, 'Go on, be as loud as you dare. Take pride in announcing your names to the world!'

Cassie filled her lungs with air and shouted at the top of her voice, 'CASSANDRA MARRAMGRASS!'

Miss Bluegrass placed a hand underneath Cassie's ribcage. 'Try breathing as deeply as you can and start the breath from here. Let the air flow through you like a sea snake on the waves. Don't try to fight it.'

Cassie surprised herself at how much louder her next shout was.

'That's much better!' said Miss Bluegrass, smiling. 'You have a lovely tone to your voice, Cassandra Marramgrass. The Marramgrass name is well regarded throughout all the dunes.'

'Is it?' Cassie asked breathlessly.

Miss Bluegrass nodded and tooted on her flute. 'It is always worth taking note of a Marramgrass – they have hidden depths.'

Miss Bluegrass beckoned everyone to gather around a large wooden crate, which she then threw open.

'Is that your crystallophone?' Ella asked as she peered into the box.

Miss Bluegrass shook her head, making all the decorations there rattle, shake or tinkle.

'What a question! I may not know much about dancing, but you seem to know even less about music. Thank goodness I came to rectify the situation and give you poor sprites a proper musical education. No, that is not a crystallophone. I am still awaiting delivery of some of the pieces so that I can assemble it and delight your ears with its fantastical sounds. After years of tinkering I have created my own special model.'

'Will it arrive in time for the Blue Moon Ballet?' Verbena asked.

'I certainly hope so – I need to start composing the music soon! Now, I want you to select an item from the box. Go on, don't be shy.'

The group kneeled down and tentatively began to take things from the jumble of objects in the crate.

'As I said before, music can be found in the most unlikely places. All these objects can be used to create a sound.'

Shell picked a large shell and began to blow it. Cassie had hung back and most of the instruments were gone when she reached the box. Right at the bottom of the crate she spied a small object made of terracotta and in the shape of a dune hopper.

'What do I do with this?' Cassie asked.

'You have to find a way to make some kind of music out of it,' Miss Bluegrass answered.

Cassie examined the small object in her hand. There did not seem to be any way to make a sound from it. She looked around the room. Everybody else, even Calluna, seemed to be making music, whether they had a bar of glass or shakers of sand. All she seemed to have was a smooth pebble. She stroked it. There was a rough section on the other side and she dragged her fingernails across it. It made a clacking sort of noise. Cassie grinned as she picked up a small wooden stick that was left in the box and began to run it up and down.

'See, Cassandra, now you are making music!' Miss Bluegrass smiled. Then she clapped her hands and yelled, 'Listen up!' Her voice seemed to quiver and change pitch as she called to them. It stopped everyone in their tracks.

'So you've found that everything has music in it, but come together and we'll see if we can't all create a harmonious piece. Don't be afraid to make a noise. Let the music pour out of you.'

'This makes a change from always being told to be quiet and follow the Rules,' Ella said to Cassie. She was clearly enjoying herself as much as Cassie was.

The result was a mix of crashes, and clicks and toots, but after a little while Cassie thought she could hear a basic sort of rhythm trying to emerge.

'I think there is some talent here at Sandringham,' Miss Bluegrass said. 'But now I want you to continue and incorporate the sounds you have created, no matter how raw and unformed they may be, with some dance steps. Do not be afraid to stomp or glide or dart or yell your little hearts out. The most important thing is to create some music and then let it guide your movements. Off we go!'

The cacophony started up again as the class picked up their instruments and twirled and swirled around the room, stomping, tapping, shrieking and dancing. The crescendo was building up to a climax when the door to the music room swung open. There stood Mrs Sandskrit, her turban trembling and her lips pursed like a giant puffa fish.

Chapter Eight

'Music resonates in the sand dancer's soul.
Dancing comes from the heart and soul.'
The Sands of Time

At first, no one noticed that the door had opened – the sand sprites were all too engrossed with stomping and moving around in a big circle making music and yelling. Calluna saw Mrs Sandskrit first and stopped stock-still. One by one the others noticed and followed suit, until there was only Ella left rattling her shell shakers along to Miss Bluegrass's glass flute.

Mrs Sandskrit didn't need to say a word – the grim look on her face said it all.

When Miss Bluegrass noticed her standing there, she stopped and smiled. 'Mrs Sandskrit, how good to see you. Have you come to join us? I think we might have some shell shakers going spare.'

Two pink circles appeared on Mrs Sandskrit's cheeks. She took a deep breath and gave a long and courteous bow before speaking in a very soft voice. 'I beg your pardon, Miss Bluegrass, I have simply called in to inform you that your class should have finished several minutes ago. Punctuality is very important at Sandringham.'

Miss Bluegrass waved her hand dismissively. 'We were having so much fun, I guess the notion of time slipped out of our creative minds and we simply forgot all about it.'

A couple of sprites giggled. They had never heard a teacher talk like this before. The rest of the class stood silent. No one wanted to get on the wrong side of their fearsome dance teacher.

Mrs Sandskrit nodded graciously, but her voice was now sounding slightly strained. 'Forgive me for interrupting your class, but Miss Youngsand Jnr is waiting for them in the science lab.' She turned round and very slowly and purposefully left the room, her scarves billowing behind her.

'I don't think those two will be performing the Sandringham Squeeze,' Shell said, as she gave her instrument one final blow before dropping it into the box.

Cassie felt torn. She had really enjoyed the music lesson, but Mrs Sandskrit was a very fine dance teacher. She was strict for a reason. More than anyone, she knew that it took a lot of discipline and self-control to become a sand dancer.

'Time to put your instrument away,' Miss Bluegrass said to Cassie, who had forgotten that she was still holding on to the terracotta dune hopper.

Miss Bluegrass closed the box of instruments and said, 'I know it's early days, but I have a kind of sixth sense about these things, and I reckon that you have a natural musicality.'

Cassie's eyes lit up. 'Oh, thank you, Miss Bluegrass. It felt strange at first, being asked to be loud and noisy. We are always being told that we have to behave with decorum, but I really enjoyed myself. It was exciting, making a noise together.'

'Making music is a sure-fire way of taking your mind off any troubles or worries.' Miss Bluegrass reached out and squeezed Cassie's arm. 'It must be hard without your mother – I've heard all about her, of course. You can always come and talk to me about anything. I am a good listener. Nothing shocks me.'

Cassie was surprised that Miss Bluegrass knew all about her, but the new teacher was so warm and friendly that Cassie did not feel offended. 'I'd like that. Sometimes I do feel a bit . . .' Cassie paused, looking for the right word.

Miss Bluegrass touched her gently on the shoulder. 'Heartsnipped is probably the word. Where I come from, we call what you're feeling right now *heartsnipped*. It's as if a bit of your heart is missing. You can never completely feel settled or happy when a loved one is not there. I feel it all the time.'

'Are you missing someone close to you too?' Cassie asked.

Miss Bluegrass let out a long heartfelt sigh. 'When you are far from home, you always miss those you have left behind. You may not see them, but they are never far from your thoughts.'

Cassie felt tears spring up in her eyes.

Miss Bluegrass handed her a handkerchief. 'Wipe your eyes. I have a strong feeling that you and I are going to become fast friends, Cassie. I for one am counting on you to show me around this place. I wouldn't admit this to everyone, but I am feeling a bit uncertain about how you sand dancers carry on. Will you help me?'

Cassie wiped her eyes and nodded.

She was sure Miss Bluegrass was about to say something else, but then Shell came back. 'Come on, Cassie, we're already late for the next class.'

Cassie waved goodbye to Miss Bluegrass and joined her friend.

'Are you all right?' Shell asked. 'You look upset.'

Cassie nodded. 'I'm fine – it's just a bit of sand in my eye.'

After the science class, Cassie and Shell went to the Secrets Cupboard – it was the only place they were sure they wouldn't be disturbed. They sprawled out on the wicker baskets.

'What a strange day! That was a crazy music lesson,' Cassie said. 'Wasn't it amazing the way Miss Bluegrass's flute changed colour?'

Shell shrugged her shoulders. 'I expect it's made out of a crystal that responds to musical pitch. What was much more amazing was seeing the expression on Mrs Sandskrit's face when she was asked if she'd like to join in!'

'She had a point though,' Cassie found herself defending Mrs Sandskrit. 'We did arrive late for our science lesson, and when it did start, everyone was fidgety and restless. There is something about stomping and yelling and banging that unsettles you. My insides feel prickled and turned over – a bit like my handkerchief after a sewing class.'

Shell shrieked. 'Don't remind me – you didn't have to stay behind and redo all your stitches. My fingers are full of needle prickles from that session.' Shell waggled her fingers.

'Still,' said Cassie slowly, 'Miss Bluegrass said that I had PO-tential,' Cassie mimicked her accent very well. 'I really like her.'

'There's something about Miss Bluegrass that doesn't feel right to me,' Shell said.

Cassie laughed. 'First you suspected Lysander was up to something, and now it's Miss Bluegrass. You are seeing spies everywhere! The visit that the Prince of Tides made to the palace has got you really rattled.'

Shell looked thoughtful. 'We know that Marina is trying to gather all the important dune dances from around the world. It's only logical that others will be searching for ways to control the forces of nature.'

'Madame Rosa invited Miss Bluegrass to come to the school, so she must have been happy about her, and checked her background,' said Cassie. She looked at Shell's face and realised she hadn't reassured her – she'd never seen Shell look so worried before. 'Besides, surf boys are always roaming about the place looking for adventures and they are by nature curious about things,' she added.

Shell nodded and said doubtfully, 'Well, I suppose we haven't seen Lysander since we saw him on the beach, so he's probably gone to Silica City, like he said.'

'We shouldn't be worrying about all this anyway,' said Cassie. 'We have to concentrate on the Blue Moon Ballet. Performing that well is something we definitely know will help the dunes.'

Shell blinked and rubbed her eyes. 'Wow, for a moment I thought Lexie was back. That's just the kind of sensible speech she would give.'

'I'm sure she would have a lot more to say about things. I do miss her,' Cassie said, 'and I hope she's getting better and not missing us too much.'

'For one thing she'd be telling us not to be late for supper.' Shell stretched her legs for one last time as she stood up. 'It was good to share those feelings with you,

Cassie. I do feel less suspicious now.'

'And I feel more suspicious, so I suppose things have evened out!' Cassie replied.

At supper time, they were all interested to see how Mrs Sandskrit and Miss Bluegrass would act around each other.

'I am hoping for a samphire bun fight at the very least!' Ella said.

But Madame Rosa sat between them, so there was no opportunity for further falling out.

Once the meal was over, Madame Rosa stood up to address the school.

'A lot of sprites have been asking about the Blue Moon Ballet auditions. You will be required to dance the sequence that we have been looking at in class and a sequence of your own choreography. The auditions will be held soon, so you will need to prepare yourselves —'

'We can look at the music to the ballet too,' Miss Bluegrass interrupted. 'It would be such fun to do some singing and music-making for the ballet performance. You never know, it might even relax everyone, and help them enjoy the musical side of the ballet as well.'

The room was silent. No one interrupted Madame Rosa – even the teachers only spoke when she invited them to. All eyes were on Madame Rosa. How was she going to treat this breach of protocol?

Madame Rosa paused, turned towards Miss

Bluegrass and curtseyed. 'Forgive me. I did not know that you wished to address the school. Thank you for your suggestion. We will certainly consider it.'

Most of the sprites began to whisper excitedly. Even Madame Rosa smiled. Only Mrs Sandskrit's frown remained.

'No sense of decorum,' Calluna tutted as they were leaving the dining hall.

'It can't be rude if you don't know how the school works, can it?' Ella asked Cassie and Shell.

'No, but maybe the polite thing to do would be to find out before you start,' Shell suggested.

As they headed off to their kutches for evening study, Miss Bluegrass caught up with Cassie. 'I was wondering if you would do me a big favour. I don't want to put my feet into things any more than I already have done. I get the impression I made a *faux pas* – a false step – just now?'

Cassie sighed. 'I suppose you did, but it wasn't your fault. You have to get used to Sandringham. Everything is very traditional here, and not as free as I think you must be used to.'

'I'll try and respect that, but it will be fun to shake things up a bit too . . . musically, I mean. Now can I trust you, Cassie, to give me the right information to help keep me out of trouble?'

Cassie nodded. 'Of course.' Cassie was amazed and

flattered that Miss Bluegrass felt she could talk so freely with her and treat her more like a friend than a pupil.

'I knew you were the best sprite!' Miss Bluegrass squeezed her arm.

Cassie blushed and mumbled, 'I wouldn't go that far.'

'So, I must never interrupt Madame Rosa at the dinner table.'

'Definitely not,' Cassie answered.

'And Thassalinus the night watchman, is he very strict too?'

'He is fierce, but you can usually win him round with a bottle of barnacle beer.'

Miss Bluegrass laughed. 'And just supposing that things get too much for me and I need to take a little air . . .'

'As a teacher you are free to move about as you please.' Cassie wondered if she should let Miss Bluegrass in on their secret, then relented. 'There are some sprite-sized peepholes on the ground floor that can give you quick access to the beach when you've got to get out, or when the gates are locked.' She pointed round the corner from where they stood in the main hall.

Miss Bluegrass nodded, taking it all in. 'I'm sure I won't be out that late, but I will need a quick way out, especially if I have an idea for a tune that needs to be free. If I can't sing when the mood takes me, I just burst!'

They reached the main staircase. 'Thank you for talking to me, Cassie,' she continued. 'You've been a real help. You'd better go off for private study, but I hope we'll chat again soon. Don't worry, your secret escape route is safe with me.'

Cassie ran up the stairs to her kutch and tried to read through the Blue Moon Ballet sequence that they had been given, but the diagrams became jumbled. She closed her eyes to visualise the dance steps. That usually helped when she was stuck, but this time there was only darkness. She couldn't shake off a sinking feeling deep inside that she had said too much. She sighed, put down the pages and went on to the balcony where she stared out at the beach.

As she breathed in the night air and watched the stars reflecting on the water, she began to feel calmer. She pushed away all her uneasy feelings about Miss Bluegrass and, when she closed her eyes the next time, she found that she could imagine the dance steps and she fell into a deep dancing dream.

Chapter Nine

'You cannot dance in another sprite's shoes.'
The Sands of Time

To her surprise, Cassie woke up really early the next morning. She'd been determined to be punctual, so she had banged her head seven times on the pillow before she went to sleep. It was one of her Aunt Euphorbia's tricks for making sure you woke up when you wanted to.

Cassie must have miscounted the number of times she'd banged her head the night before, because she had woken up at six, an hour earlier than necessary. She stood on the balcony and sniffed the air. It was the most beautiful morning with a pearly, pale winter sun and a light sea breeze.

To pass the time, she slowly washed and dressed. She tried to do her hair in the new double-bun style, but it just didn't look right on her, so she put in the usual simple marramgrass twists in her braids instead.

But there was still lots of time before breakfast.

She thought about waking up Shell. *No, she is so grumpy if she is disturbed. Besides I'm not sure I can face wisecracks or conversation this early in the morning*, Cassie told herself. *A walk on the beach will calm me down.*

She threw on her green winter cloak, climbed down the balcony ladder and walked quickly to the beach.

Cassie enjoyed the feeling of the cool, moist sea breeze and the way it tossed and pulled her braids. *It would be nice to carry around the tang of the beach throughout the day*, she thought.

As she padded towards her favourite spot, she slowed her steps, seeing swirls and footprints in the sand ahead. Someone had got there before her. Who could it be? Cassie crept closer and watched the sprite dance.

It was really wonderful. All the seven basic steps fused beautifully together. As soon as the exercise was complete, Cassie couldn't help but clap.

Lysander spun round. He was breathing heavily from the dancing and his long dark curls were heavy with sweat, even though the morning was cold. He reached into his belt and pulled out a cloth to wipe his face. 'If it isn't one of the nameless sand dancers,' he said to her. 'Only this time, *you* are sneaking up on *me*.'

'I thought you were in Silica City,' Cassie said, walking towards him. 'Besides, you are wearing out my favourite practice spot. You dance really well. Where did you learn all the steps?'

'You and your snippy friend aren't the only dancers who practise on the beach.'

'I don't think Shell would take kindly to being called snippy,' Cassie answered sharply.

Lysander bowed. 'Please accept my humble apologies. I did not mean to be rude. In fact, I like sand sprites with a bit of spirit. It makes life more interesting. And I do appreciate your comments on my dancing.'

Cassie curtseyed slightly, accepting his apology.

'I picked up those steps watching you the other day. I have always found dancing a good way of clearing my head,' Lysander said. 'I often dance, particularly if I'm in a strange place. Travelling is fun, but sometimes you find yourself so far away from home that it hurts.' Lysander looked ahead at the rolling sea, and sighed.

'I know that feeling,' Cassie replied.

'Are you feeling homesick too?' Lysander asked eagerly.

'Not homesick exactly, because Sandringham feels like home to me. I suppose it's family and friends that I am missing.'

'You're feeling heartsnipped,' Lysander said.

'That's the word!' Cassie replied. 'Miss Bluegrass used that word too.' She paused shyly. 'You actually remind me a bit of a friend of mine. Are you any good at throwing pebbles? I am very good at beating surf boys in pebble-throwing competitions.'

Lysander shook his head. 'You'd whoop me easily at that – I am hopeless at throwing pebbles. Why don't we dance together instead. You can see if I have these moves right?'

He unwound some rope from around his wrist and tied his long black hair back, and without giving Cassie a chance to refuse, assumed a starting position, saying, 'You lead and I'll follow.'

Cassie hesitated for a moment. This was against so many Rules . . . but she remembered that he had watched her mother dance and, in a strange sort of a way, dancing with him would make a connection with her.

She began carefully at first, making her movements slow and sure, easy to copy – a long sweep of the pointed foot, an arching gesture of the arms – and soon they fell into an easy, silent rhythm, moving in unison together as the sea breeze danced around their steps.

After they had been through the seven basic dance steps a few times, Cassie began to improvise, and speed up a little, to see what Lysander would do. He smiled at the change in pace, and would take the lead a little, and then, after a while, it was hard to tell who was leading who as they were dancing together in perfect harmony.

'Imagine we are Blown By The Wind jellyfish, first swimming and then flying through the air,' he said, as he lifted Cassie by the waist and twirled her around.

'Whee! It does feel like I am flying,' Cassie screamed

as she held the Dune Arabesque, in mid-air.

'Hold steady and concentrate! You have to trust me. I won't let you fall!' Lysander ordered and he shifted his weight until they were balanced again. 'Fear makes you heavy,' he said.

'Then I shall think about blades of marramgrass wafting in the sea breeze!' Cassie said.

'Just not too many of them,' Lysander joked as he twirled her one last time before he carefully placed her back down on the sand.

They stood in a rest position, regaining their breath.

'Could you tell me some more about the night you saw Marina Marramgrass dance?' Cassie asked him eventually.

Lysander sighed. 'It is hard for me to talk about it, because when I do, strong memories race back into my mind again and stir me up. Does that ever happen to you?'

Cassie nodded. 'If I think about the Night of the Great Sandstorm and how I got lost, even though it was years ago, my heart still pounds. Sometimes I dream that I am stuck in the middle of a sandstorm and it is such a relief to wake up and realise that I am not alone any more, but that I am at dance school and I'm safe.'

Lysander sat down and drew his knees up to his chest. 'It seems that the Night of the Great Sandstorm changed everything. Sometimes I wish that we could all forget about it.' He uncurled his legs and stretched out his arms. 'And then there are some memories that are so delicious that you don't want to think about them too much in case they get worn out.'

'Or, if you tell them to the wrong person, it can feel that you squandered a memory,' Cassie exclaimed. 'I get that feeling sometimes when I talk about dancing to my aunt.'

Lysander sighed wistfully. 'It's awful trying to talk about what dancing means to you to someone who doesn't really understand, no matter how much they care about you. You are very lucky being at Sandringham. You can talk to any sprite there and they will be on the same wavelength. Was it very hard to get a place?'

Cassie nodded. 'There were auditions, which were really tough. Sandrine, the Supreme Sand Sprite was there, which made it doubly scary.'

'Not as scary as trying to explain to the Prince of Tides why you have bruised a jellyfish! I met him once a few years ago. He is so fierce if any sea creatures are not properly looked after.' Lysander shuddered. Then he asked, 'Can anyone audition for Sandringham?'

Cassie shrugged. 'I'm not really sure.'

'But there are no surf boys there?' he asked.

Cassie giggled. 'No way! I don't think there ever have been.' She blinked as the sun shone into her face, then she sprang to her feet. 'Look at the time! I am going to be late after all! You'll have to tell me about how my mother danced another time.'

'Your mother! Marina Marramgrass is your mother?' Lysander's voice rose up a pitch.

Cassie blushed. She hadn't meant to let the news slip out like that. 'Yes, she is my mother.'

Lysander pinched his arms. 'I don't believe it! I have been dancing with . . . I don't even know your name.'

'Cassandra, but I'm usually called Cassie.'

Lysander bowed. 'I am deeply honoured to have met and danced with you, Cassandra Marramgrass.' He paused. 'Do you think we could dance again some time? You are an amazing sand dancer. I could learn a lot from you.'

Cassie felt her cheeks go hot. 'You're only saying that because of my mother.'

'We danced together before I knew your name,' Lysander pointed out. 'Besides, I have never danced a duet with anyone before. I did try it with a jellyfish once, but it didn't work out.'

Cassie giggled again. 'I really have to go. See you around, Lysander.' And without another word, she raced back to school.

There was just enough time to splash her face with cold water, pick up her exercises book and make her way to Mrs Sandskrit's class. She had to skip breakfast in order to stand any chance of being on time.

She ran straight over to the practice room. She opened the door carefully and prepared her bow of apology. The door creaked open. The room was empty. Cassie's footsteps echoed across the floor. Where was the class? There must have been an announcement at breakfast! What was she going to do now?

She headed towards the music room to see if Miss Bluegrass knew what had happened to everyone, but there was no one in her room either. She walked back along the corridor to Miss Youngsand's science lab, but that was empty too. A creak on the floorboards made her stop. Feeling hot and unsettled, she walked towards the noise and backed into Thassalinus, who was sweeping the corridor.

'Aargh!' they both yelled.

Thassalinus dropped his broom. 'Slippery sea slugs, you nearly parted me from my breakfast! If you don't get a move on down to the grotto you're going to be late for the —'

Cassie did not wait to hear any more – she was off skidding down the corridor and doubling back on herself to get to the grotto as fast as her feet would carry her, snagging an embroidered panel of her practice dress on a bush by the swimming pool. She groaned as she felt the delicate material tear, but there was no time to stop.

Madame Rosa was not impressed. 'We were just about to start without you.'

'I am so sorry . . .' Cassie blurted out her apology in between gulps for air.

'I expect you overslept. You are not the only one, but

you are the last to arrive. Please do not make a habit of it.'

Mrs Sandskrit, who was standing beside her, draped in a maroon cape, pursed her lips. 'And take more care of your grooming in future. There is a tear in your skirt. What have you been up to? Racing on the beach or wrestling with sea slugs?'

Everyone laughed and Cassie wished she could dive into the fountain and disappear. Instead, she just hung her head and whispered, 'I won't ever be late again.'

Madame Rosa hushed the sprites and began. 'As I explained at breakfast, I have brought you down here this morning to show you a special lantern show of the Blue Moon Ballet. I thought it would inspire you all to work hard for the auditions which we will be holding in the next few weeks.'

A ripple of excitement went through the sprites. They were sitting around the shell sculpture looking at the back wall. There were only a few precious viewing lanterns that had not been broken up and destroyed during the Great Sandstorm and even fewer images of sand dancers performing.

Miss Youngsand Snr, who was operating the lantern, said, 'Settle down, sand dancers, and pay full attention. These few images that I am about to show you are the only record of a performance of the Blue Moon Ballet.'

Madame Rosa stood by Cassie and whispered, 'I was hoping to catch you before the class to warn you that this will include some images of your mother dancing, so prepare yourself.'

The glass strips whirled round the lantern, and the images projected on to the wall in rapid succession, so it appeared the cast images were moving. They were hard to make out clearly, though, because the ballet had been danced by the light of the moon and flickering torch-light, but the dune dancers performed a beautiful sequence of complex jumps, lifts and twirls that the sprites had never seen before, and which made Madame Rosa's previous classes look easy.

'This next strip will show the prima dune dancer's solo spot. This is the section we will be replacing with a group dance and a musical interlude,' Madame Rosa announced. Cassie took a large gulp of air and squeezed her hands tightly in her lap.

'Once you have seen this, I think you will realise why the Blue Moon Ballet is so special and why it will need lots of extra dance practice even to get close to performing it well,' Mrs Sandskrit said.

All the sprites held their breath and sat up really straight, eager to catch a glimpse of Marina Marramgrass dancing the Blue Moon solo.

The next image came up, but it seemed to be out of sequence – it was a slide of a very young girl dancing. The outfit she was wearing was old-fashioned and the colours were faded. And yet there was something very beautiful about the girl, her legs even longer and more flexible than Marina's. There was something vaguely familiar about her, but, before Cassie could think why, Miss Youngsand Snr had removed the glass strip saying, 'Oh dear, that shouldn't be there. It's an old strip that must have got mixed in.'

'Where were you?' Shell whispered, seizing the opportunity to quiz Cassie. 'And don't say you overslept, because I called for you and there was no sign of you when I peeped in your kutch.'

'I woke up early and went for a walk on the beach where I lost track of the time,' Cassie said.

Shell gave her one of her *I don't believe you* looks and said, 'We'll talk later.'

Cassie frowned. Should she tell her friend about meeting Lysander and dancing a dune duet? Part of her was bursting to tell Shell, but another part felt that it would only make her suspicious and angry again.

'The lantern is now reset,' Miss Youngsand Snr said.

'Watch it carefully,' Madame Rosa ordered. 'All the previous moves and dance steps have been building up to this moment. It is the high point of the ballet. After the prima dune dancer has performed this sequence, the dunes should begin to sing, and the other dune dancers join her to perform the final sequences. At this moment all the attention and responsibility is on Marina Marramgrass.'

Cassie felt her skin prickle as she watched her mother dance the solo spot. Her movements were complex and demanding, but she performed with such lightness and delicacy that it seemed that she was dancing a duet with the moonbeams. Sometimes it looked as if she was being controlled and pulled along by the moon and then, with a wave of her hand and a point of her toes, she seemed to scoop up the moonbeams in her arms and dance with them. Marina's face glowed with happiness. She made it look effortless.

Chapter Ten

'A sand lion does not give you a second chance.'
The Sands of Time

From that moment on, everyone was obsessed by the Blue Moon Ballet. It was the only topic of conversation. Everyone tried to sneak the colour blue into their practice outfits or weave a blue flower into their hair. There were new dance steps to learn such as Space Shuffles, Earthshines, Planetary Pirouettes and Eclipses.

Ella stunned everyone by dyeing her hair blue. She thought it was funny until she tried to wash it out. 'Squid ink is pretty permanent,' Miss Youngsand Snr told her, and Miss Youngsand Jnr had to go to the science lab to mix up a special shampoo, which got rid of the blue, but left Ella's hair with green streaks.

Every spare moment was taken up with preparing for the audition. The sprites became very secretive about what they were going to do to fill in the missing section, but a lot of practising could be heard from their kutches in the evening, and a lot of dancers rehearsed in secret parts of the school when they were sure no one was watching them. Everyone wanted to impress Mrs Sandskrit with their own ideas and dancing skills. As well as being secretive, a lot of sprites also became suspicious of each other and arguments broke out as they accused each other of copying or spying.

Cassie had found a secluded area on the ground floor corridor, which allowed her plenty of space to dance. She was trying to find a way to combine the Sand Stretch with a Sand Glide, since she felt she could perform those movements the best. She often found the peepholes down there open to the beach, and she enjoyed the lift the breezes gave her.

One morning she even startled Miss Bluegrass, who was pacing up and down the corridors.

'Oh, Cassie, am I glad to see you.' She waved a sheet of the Blue Moon Ballet. 'Can you just explain this sequence of dance steps for me?'

'Are you going to audition for a part then?' Cassie joked.

Miss Bluegrass looked offended, stuck her chin out and said in a fierce voice, 'I found this in my classroom and naturally assumed it was for me, but maybe a sprite had just left it behind. Either way I am trying to compose some music and it would really help me out to know some of the steps. They are not a secret, are they?' She held out the paper accusingly to Cassie.

Cassie was a little taken aback by her reaction and said, 'The dance steps are special and shouldn't be passed around lightly, but you are a trusted member of staff.'

Miss Bluegrass blushed. 'That is kind of you.'

Cassie looked down at the paper and noticed that one of the corners had been folded back in a certain way and a doodle of a conch shell was drawn in the corner. 'This belongs to Shell,' she said. 'She must have left it after the music lesson. I'll take it for her.'

'Don't worry,' said Miss Bluegrass. 'I'll give it to her.'

It was fun teaching the steps and the sequence to Miss Bluegrass.

'I'm hopeless at this,' Miss Bluegrass wailed. 'I can't seem to get the hang of it. I need a song to help me remember.'

So Cassie made up some words:

'The Earthshine is a step so fine
Stretch your legs and extend your arms
Use your charms to make yourself look
Like the old moon in the new moon's arms.'

'You have a real talent for writing songs.' Miss Bluegrass fanned herself with the paper. Thank you for showing me the steps. I really appreciate it.'

* * *

So another two weeks passed. As Cassie was practising in the corridor one afternoon, Thassalinus found her and pushed a piece of paper into her hand saying, 'If you want my opinion she is still looking peaky. And stop leaving the windows open in this corridor. Any sprite could walk in here!'

'I never open —' started Cassie, but Thassalinus had already gone. She looked at the letter in her hand and smiled. What perfect timing to hear from Lexie. She had just been wishing she could have a long chat with her about technique and ideas for the audition.

Cassie raced back to her kutch to read it.

Dear Cassie,

It was so wonderful to get your letter, and funny, because it arrived on the day that your Aunt Euphorbia paid me a visit. She sends her regards and hopes that you are working hard and staying out of trouble! As if!

She has been really kind to me. She brought some tonic ointment for my legs and has given me some strengthening exercises to build up the muscle tone. She told me that she was about my age when she hurt her leg. But of course you know all about that.

I'm really sorry I didn't let you know that I wasn't coming back for the start of term, but I suppose I kept on hoping that my leg would heal in time.

Anyway, the good news is that I am slowly getting better, which is great, because I am desperate to be back at

Sandringham. I have to spend a lot of my time resting, which is really driving me crazy. I am keeping busy by learning lots of new recipes as I watch my mother make her sea cakes. I have even dreamed up a new dish – I call it the white horses omelette. I can't wait to make it for you sometime. Tell Shell that I hope she hasn't got a mountain of sewing for me to do. Her hairstyle sounds very peculiar, or has she changed it back? Tell me more about the music lessons!

Please, please write back if you can. I am longing to hear all the news about the Blue Moon Ballet. Isn't it wonderful that we will get the chance to be a part of it? My mother has been showing me all the steps, so with a bit of luck I might be able to catch up. I am going to try my hardest to. I better end this letter here, as Thassalinus has finished eating all the sea cakes that Mother has been feeding him and is beginning to grumble.

Big friendship hug to you and all at Sandringham.

Lexie.

Cassie read the letter three times and each time she came to the bit about Euphorbia, she was taken aback. Her aunt had not mentioned in her letters to Cassie that she'd been to see Lexie. Nor had she ever told her that she had injured her leg when she was a young sand sprite. Cassie had just assumed that Aunt Euphorbia's leg had always been like that. Sprites were always confiding in Lexie, Cassie realised, because she was such a good listener. She couldn't help feeling a little miffed, though, that her aunt had told Lexie, but not her.

It took a long time for Cassie to get to sleep that night – she felt restless and had some strange dreams. She was in the middle of dreaming that she was swimming through a white horse omelette, when she woke up with a start. Someone was in her room. She sat up at the same time as an icy hand grabbed her.

Cassie opened her mouth to scream, but just at that moment, she realised that it was only a freezing cold Ella. Cassie wrapped her blanket round Ella's shoulders.

Ella trembled. 'Oh, Cassie, I think I have just seen a ghost.' She took some big gulps of air. 'I thought I would do some extra practice – I was desperate to see how well I could dance by moonlight. I crept down to the beach, but there was a mist and the light was not good. I did a few dance steps and decided to come straight back. As I was turning to go, I suddenly realised that I wasn't alone – I saw a figure dancing in the mist. When I turned to look again it had vanished. I was so frightened.'

'Don't be frightened. Perhaps another sand dancer had the same idea as you.'

'That's the strange part!' wailed Ella. 'I couldn't be sure, but it looked like a surf boy!'

Cassie's breath caught in her throat. Could she risk telling Ella all about Lysander? Of course, she thought, but then she had not even told Shell about dancing the duet with him and Shell would be hurt if Ella knew and she didn't. She decided against it for the moment.

'I wouldn't worry, Ella. When you are sleepy, your mind tries to trick your eyes,' Cassie suggested.

Ella considered this, and then nodded. 'I am finding it hard to keep my eyes open – perhaps they *are* playing tricks on me. Thank you, Cassie.' She got up to go, but turned back at the doorway. 'I think my mind is full with everything that's going on here. I didn't tell you the weirdest thing – it looked like he was dancing part of the Blue Moon Ballet!'

Once Ella had gone, Cassie felt more and more worried. The mysterious surf boy must be Lysander, but where had he learned the steps? Was it possible that maybe, just maybe, when they were dancing together, she had shown him some of the steps? Had she accidentally given away some of the secrets of the sand dancers?

Chapter Eleven

'Hurling angry, hurtful words
is like throwing sand into the wind:
it always blows right back again.'
The Sands of Time

'Shell, just for once will you take this seriously?' Cassie hissed at her friend during their next music lesson. 'You are supposed to be humming and holding the note for as long as possible. Not pulling fish faces.'

'It hurts my lips!' Shell insisted. 'They've gone numb.'

'You're not trying hard enough,' Cassie snapped. There were only three more days to go to the audition and everyone was getting tense and edgy.

'All my energy is taken up with trying to get those tricky Blue Moon Ballet combinations right. And don't even talk to me about that individual section. Are my steps good enough? Are they clever enough? My head is spinning with it all!' Shell grumbled as she patted her lips. 'And if you weren't Miss Bluegrass's pet sprite you wouldn't be taking this music so seriously.'

'There is nothing wrong with developing musical ability, and I am *not* Miss Bluegrass's pet sprite. You're just saying that because you don't like her for some reason,' Cassie replied.

'Some reason?' Shell snorted. 'I have lot of reasons why I don't trust her. She's a stranger. We know nothing about her. She just happened to find my sheet from the Blue Moon Ballet. Miss Bluegrass . . .' muttered Shell. 'Miss Blue-Snake-in-the-Grass, more like! And did I tell you I've seen her creeping about the school after lights-out on a couple of occasions now? And she is always hanging around the peepholes that we use to escape to the beach.'

'Perhaps she wants to spend more time in the music room,' suggested Cassie. Now was certainly not the time to admit to Shell that she had told Miss Bluegrass that the peepholes were the best way to escape to the beach. 'What were you doing after lights-out?'

'Sneaking a few extra sea pasties from the kitchen,' replied Shell. 'I've been getting really nervous with this audition, and when I'm nervous, I eat.'

'If you listened more to the music part of it, you'd feel more relaxed, and you might find that you enjoyed it too,' Cassie said sharply.

'And I wish that you wouldn't be so easily taken in by

a few compliments!' Shell replied. 'It's sickening the way you suck up to Miss Bluegrass. You are so impressionable sometimes, Cassie.' Shell glared back at her.

Just at that moment, Ella walked past them, wearing two crystal flutes in her large coiled braids.

Cassie put on her best Shell voice. 'Now that is what I call impressionable!' And they both laughed and their crossness with each other began to disappear for the moment.

'What's up?' Ella turned round, looking a bit hurt. 'Are you laughing at me?'

'Not really. We are trying to stop ourselves from having a huge argument with each other,' Cassie said.

Ella nodded. 'I suppose we are all a bit tetchy before an audition. I have been experimenting with my hair to take my mind off things. You know what we need . . .'

They chanted together, 'All you need is a Sandringham Squeeze.'

'Shall we get everybody involved?' asked Cassie. 'I'm sure Miss Bluegrass wouldn't mind.'

Shell rolled her eyes, but Cassie was already moving across the room.

Miss Bluegrass thought it was a 'mighty fine' idea and called the class together. They formed a circle and passed the squeeze saying,

'Sandringham Squeeze, Sandringham Squeeze
Loyal and true till the oceans freeze.

Follow the dance steps from seven to one
You may take a little rest
After a Dune Arabesque
And take a lot of pride
In doing the perfect Sand Glide.
There's so much we can achieve
Sand dancing together
Floating along on a light sea breeze
You'll always find a friend
With a Sandringham Squeeze.'

Miss Bluegrass sang out the words too. When she had finished she whispered with a sad smile, 'Loyal and true – indeed, they are noble qualities.'

Then she shook her head firmly, making a light tinkling sound, as she said in a big loud voice, 'That was wonderful, but next time we are going to sing it and I will accompany you on the crystallophone. Thassalinus delivered the final crate today. I can now assemble it in time for our next lesson, so you can hear it before the audition. Anyway, there is just enough time left for our final wind-down. You must not be late for your next class. Mrs Sandskrit was right when she said it is important to keep an eye on the time. We must be *Loyal and true till the oceans freeze.'*

Miss Bluegrass stood in the middle of the sprite circle. She raised her arms up and then placed them on her abdomen.

'Start with a deep low vibration and slowly raise it – deep breath, everyone, and let's go. We are aiming to be as loud as we can!'

The noise level reached an impressive volume before Miss Bluegrass, in the role of conductor, made a flourish with her hand to signal for them to be quiet. They could all hear the sound of Mrs Sandskrit's voice outside the door.

'See, Madame Rosa! That is not music, it is just pure din. It's rattling Miss Youngsand Jnr's test tubes and it is shaking my nerves!'

All the sprites looked at Miss Bluegrass in sympathy. For a split second, it seemed as if she was about to cry, but in a flash she had recovered and was back to her smiling self. 'We'd better end there for today.'

As she passed her on the way out, Cassie tried to lighten the mood, saying, 'We are really looking forward to hearing the crystallophone.'

'It does make a fine *din*,' Miss Bluegrass agreed pointedly as they all filed out.

'I don't like all this tension. It has been building up for weeks. Nobody wants to share their dance routines for fear that someone else will copy them. You and Shell were arguing in class earlier on, and now Miss Bluegrass is upset and Mrs Sandskrit is cross. It's making my tummy ache,' Ella complained over lunch.

'Mrs Sandskrit and Miss Bluegrass have different

ways of teaching us, that's all,' Cassie said.

'It's what Sandrine calls competing interests.' Shell reached for some laver bread.

'But music helps me with my dancing. There is no competition for me,' Ella replied.

'In a way, we are all in competition with each other, though, aren't we?' Cassie chewed thoughtfully.

'Cassie's right. We all want to be the best dancer in the school and only one of us can be,' Shell said. 'At the moment, we all want to be good enough to be in the select group.'

'Lexie is probably the best sand dancer,' Ella pointed out.

'You are only as good as your last audition,' said Calluna from across the table. 'We'll see what Lexie is made of when she returns. She'll definitely be out of condition. Besides she may not be right for a lead part in the Blue Moon Ballet. Madame Rosa was very clear when she said that selection would not be based solely on technical ability, but on a talent for dancing in harmony with the blue moon. Lexie might not be good at that.'

'Now I do feel a Rage Stomp coming on,' Cassie said through gritted teeth. 'How dare she talk about Lexie like that.' Cassie raised her voice so that Calluna could hear. 'I hope Lexie comes back and gets the best part.'

'My feelings are surging like an angry wave. What is happening to us?' Ella asked.

'What we need is a good fight to clear the air,' Shell

said as she slurped her seaweed soup.

'Come to think of it, my toes haven't itched with anger like this in a long time,' Cassie said. 'Listening to Calluna's opinion of Lexie has really got me going. Not to mention the fact that I am probably a bit jealous of Lexie's natural dancing ability myself.'

'There is a lot of pressure on you because you are the prima dune dancer's daughter.' Ella smiled encouragingly.

Cassie put down her spoon and looked at her friends. 'We may be in competition with each other, but that doesn't mean we can't still help each other. Who's up for an extra Blue Moon Ballet practice tomorrow? We can watch and correct each other. Faults are much easier to see in other people and we can put them right without yelling like the Sand Dragon! We don't need to show our original moves, but we can practise the rest of the ballet.'

'Brilliant idea!' Ella said. 'Even better than doing a Rage Stomp!'

'Count me in too,' added Shell. 'I feel like I have two left feet when it comes to the Planetary Pirouette.'

Cassie smiled and looked up at the teachers' table, and to Miss Bluegrass and Mrs Sandskrit practically sitting back to back to each other now. 'If only everyone could get on like we do,' she said, nodding towards them. 'The practical problem that we are faced with is that our music lesson disturbs everyone else and stops them from doing their work.'

'Then Mrs Sandskrit gets cross and comes marching

in with all her robes and scarves flying about the place. She needs to muffle her emotions,' replied Ella, scooping up her bowl and finishing off the last of her soup.

'Ella, you're a genius!' Cassie banged her hand so hard on the table that Ella nearly ended up wearing the soup bowl as a hat. 'Meet me in the Secrets Cupboard after school. And wear some old clothes.'

'It won't take long, will it? I need my beauty sleep to prepare for the coming audition,' Ella replied.

'And just how old do you want the clothes to be?' Shell asked.

Cassie gritted her teeth. 'Doodlebug! We are going to have a night of constructive mischief which will do us and hopefully everybody else the world of good.'

Chapter Twelve

*'The most beautiful music can be made
from out of silence.'*
The Sands of Time

Everyone was amazed when they walked into the music room the next day.

'It's like a velvet cave!' Verbena said, as she touched the walls that were now draped with heavy curtains. Then she coughed as a cloud of dust flew up.

'It's like a dream come true,' Miss Bluegrass said, beaming. 'The room is soundproofed now, so we can make as much noise as we like without upsetting any-one. I was so delighted when I came in this morning to set up the crystallophone.'

'I heard a rumour that the soundproofing was Mrs Sandskrit's idea,' Cassie said as she winked at Shell.

'Then straight after the lesson I must go and thank

her. Now I would like to demonstrate the Bluegrass Crystallophone. I have adapted the standard model with a few secret tweaks of my own to create this unique instrument. It is going to create some celestial sand tunes to inspire the dunes by the light of the moon!'

She beckoned them over to the middle of the room where three tables stood covered with a large cloth. Miss Bluegrass carefully lifted it and the sprites gathered round for their first glimpse of the constructed crystallophone.

'You have already been practising with the crystal flutes, but now it is time to unveil this! Over the past few weeks I have been attempting to help you discover your voice and help you find rhythm and harmony. Now it gives me great pleasure to perform for you on my beloved customised crystallophone. You may see other crystallophones, but you will never hear one that sounds quite like my instrument.' She stood behind the tables and stroked the edges of the glass. 'Being separated from this has been like being separated from a dear friend.'

The first table had a series of glass bowls filled with water on it. The tables on either side had long pieces of glass resting on driftwood bases. Miss Bluegrass picked up some wooden sticks and began to tap lightly on the long pieces of glass, sending out ripples of sounds. Then she waved her fingers over the rims of the glass bowls and a series of haunting sounds filled the room. Her expression, for once, was serious as she concentrated on

109

producing the sounds. As she played and nodded her head, it seemed that her headdress became a part of the instrument too.

The room filled with the beautiful sounds and vibrations. After a few moments, Cassie felt her wings vibrate and her toes began to tingle. The sounds were so enchanting and inviting that she simply had to dance. Tentatively she stretched out her arms and pointed her toes. When she looked around, she could see that the other sand dancers were also starting to strike dance poses spontaneously. The music was making them dance.

'Music acts like a force compelling you to dance. It drags you along with it. Like the moon and the tide, we have a constant relationship.'

Soon the whole room was filled with dancing and the fluttering of wings. As the final note quivered and died the dancing also stopped and the class realised that they were not alone.

This time Mrs Sandskrit was speechless with amazement as she came into the room. Eventually she said, 'I beg your pardon for interrupting, but as there was no noise blaring out from the room I thought something might be wrong.'

Miss Bluegrass raised her fingers from the crystallophone and winked knowingly at Mrs Sandskrit. 'It's the curtains, you clever thing. They have certainly done the trick! I hope you were careful with those wooden boxes.'

She pointed over at the wooden crates with *Bluegrass* written on them that were neatly stacked in a corner.

Mrs Sandskrit looked embarrassed and said, 'I don't know what you are talking about, but please don't stop playing on my account. The sounds were exquisite and absolutely perfect for dancing. It was truly inspirational and will be a wonderful addition to the Blue Moon Ballet. I see now what Madame Rosa meant when she said that certain sounds could enhance our dancing.'

Miss Bluegrass gave an uncharacteristic blush and bowed graciously, the silver bells in her hair tinkling gently. 'That is the power of my crystallophone.'

Cassie could see that she was both pleased and unsettled by Mrs Sandskrit's comments. *I wonder why she's so confused*, she thought.

Then Mrs Sandskrit gathered herself and spoke in her usual voice. 'I have come with an important announcement. In preparation for the auditions for the Blue Moon Ballet tomorrow night, all lessons, after this one, today and tomorrow will be cancelled.'

A cheer rose from the class.

Mrs Sandskrit tried to keep a straight face. 'You will be expected to use that time to prepare your unique dance pieces, and also to sleep. Tomorrow night, the auditions will take place on a stretch of beach on the edge of Dreamy Dune, close to where we are building the stage for the actual ballet.'

'How thrilling!' Miss Bluegrass made a shimmering

noise from the crystallophone.

Mrs Sandskrit continued. 'Tonight, after supper, there will be a practice session in the courtyard, to get you used to dancing by moonlight. I suggest you have a sleep this afternoon so that you are not too tired to perform. Work hard and do your best, and don't forget to wear your cloaks this evening.' She smiled encouragingly at everyone before she left.

It was hard to concentrate after that news, so Miss Bluegrass played a lively tune and everyone swirled and twirled around the room until they had got some of the excitement out of their systems and felt settled enough to continue with their music lesson, and Miss Bluegrass told them to see how the crystallophone could better their dance steps.

It felt strange to go to their kutches while there was still daylight outside. Shell and Cassie couldn't help but pause by Lexie's empty kutch.

'Poor Lexie, she doesn't even know about the Blue Moon Ballet,' Shell sighed.

Cassie looked down at her feet. 'As a matter of fact she does. Thassalinus delivered a letter for me and I've got a reply.'

Shell's cheeks flushed an angry red. 'And you never thought to tell me? I might have wanted to add a line. That was a bit selfish. Or did you think I would butt in?' Shell's feet stomped.

Cassie's toes began to itch with rage too, and her braids began to swish. 'It wasn't like that. It was a spur-of-the-moment thing.'

'I just wish you'd told me, that's all,' Shell said in a hurt voice. 'Sometimes I feel on the edge of the friend-ship between you and Lexie. I would have liked to have written to her.'

Cassie pinched her friend's arm. 'Don't be silly. We are all best friends together. Although, as you know, sometimes I do feel jealous of Lexie's dancing ability. I was happy to tell her about Lysander —'

'What's to tell? We met him once on the beach. That's all there is to it.'

Cassie squirmed a bit. 'I did meet him again once more, and we went through some dance steps together. In fact, we danced a dune duet. He is an amazing dancer. I haven't seen him since, but sometimes I get this feeling that he is not very far away. He is desperate to become a sand dancer.'

'Cassandra Marramgrass, you never cease to amaze me – and that is why I suppose you are one of my best friends.' Shell shook her head. 'And I can't have another argument with you so soon after our argument about Miss Bluegrass and just before our audition.'

'It is hard to think badly of a sprite that can create such dreamy music. Her crystallophone literally made me dance,' Cassie sighed.

'Don't forget what she has been up to, sneaking about

113

the place and pumping you for information,' Shell reminded her. 'I intend to keep a close eye on her, and you should too.'

'My feelings sometimes get in the way of doing the right thing. I very nearly didn't tell Lexie about the Blue Moon Ballet, because I thought that, if there was no reason for her to hurry back right away, it would give me a better chance of getting into the select group.' She looked at Shell. 'I don't feel proud of that, and it isn't something I would just tell anybody about.' A tear slid down Cassie's cheek.

Shell hugged her friend. 'And I am sorry for being jealous of your friendship with Lexie. I guess we've all been a little preoccupied with the ballet, and a bit too worried about the auditions tomorrow! Anyway, I want to hear all about this so-called dune duet that you danced.'

'The best bit was when Lysander lifted me up. I truly felt as if I was flying. I'm sorry I kept it from you,' Cassie said. 'I was getting fed up of you always criticising me for liking Miss Bluegrass.'

'And I am sorry I snapped at you. But I still can't shake off my suspicious feelings about Miss Blue-Snake-in-the-Grass.'

'Let's stop saying sorry,' said Cassie. 'If we carry on like this, we'll never get enough sleep for tonight's practice!'

Chapter Thirteen

'The dance is always more important
than the sand dancer.'
The Sands of Time

The night of the audition had arrived at last! Cassie woke up to see a bright full moon through her peep-hole. The practice session the night before had seemed dreamy, the class going through the ballet sequences with Madame Rosa in the moonlit courtyard. Tonight would be different: everybody would be in competition with one another.

Splashing lots of cold water on her face and bend-ing and stretching her legs helped to wake her up. Her tummy bubbled with excitement as she dressed and checked over the Blue Moon Ballet section that they had all been given.

At first, when Cassie stared at the page, it was as if

she was looking at it for the very first time again. None of it made any sense to her. Panic rose in her throat. She paced around the room taking deep breaths and doing some of the breathing exercises that Miss Bluegrass had taught them. She went to the balcony and let out a low deep hum that seemed to vibrate through her body and make her feel calmer.

When she looked at the page of dance moves again, she remembered them.

Then she looked at the section that had been left blank for the dancers to put in their own improvised part. She walked through the intricate pattern of steps that she had prepared, which now finished with a Double Silica Jump.

'It still doesn't feel right,' she whispered to herself. 'And it has to impress Madame Rosa and Mrs Sandskrit.' She sat down on the bed once more and dropped her head in her hands.

What can I do to impress them? she asked herself. *What would my mother do?* She lay back for a moment and closed her eyes. She found herself remembering the lantern show. What had been the most amazing part of her mother's solo? Was it the way that her dance interacted with the moonlight, or the way she pointed and swept her toes? Cassie sighed. It didn't matter. She could never execute those dance moves – it would take many more years of training.

I had better stop thinking about how to impress and

focus on what I can do well. Cassie thought back to her audition last term and how she had been made to respond to the sounds that she had heard in the shell headdress. Channelling her emotions into her dancing was something that came naturally to her.

Cassie also found herself recalling something that Miss Youngsand Snr had told them about the ballet: *The ballet is all about looking back and regretting and wishing for a better life ahead.*

Slowly an idea began to form as Cassie dressed. By the time she was ready, she was smiling, and placed the slightly crumpled and tear-stained piece of paper on the bed and made her way down to the main entrance.

Miss Youngsand Snr was already there, handing out flaming torches to light the way. 'There is a chill in the air so keep moving,' she ordered.

At the far edge of Dreamy Dune, a circle of shells had been arranged to mark out the performance area, with a flickering torch in each shell to light it. Miss Bluegrass was seated with her crystallophone in a separate shell circle.

Ella stood beside Cassie, waving her torch dangerously close to her. 'Careful,' Cassie said, ducking as Ella's torch came near.

'Sorry – I'm just so excited,' Ella explained as Cassie and Shell let her walk on ahead of them.

'It's safer that way!' Shell joked.

Cassie's heart was racing, while at the same time her mind was slowing down. For the second time that night, she couldn't seem to remember the dance steps that she had been practising so hard over the preceding weeks. Once again they had danced right out of her head.

She froze and looked up at the large yellow moon in the sky.

I can't do this, she thought as panic gripped her. Then a gust of cool wind rippled around her face and ruffled her cloak. Her toes itched and she stomped on that thought and replaced it with another one. *I am going to try! I am going to take a deep breath and do my best!*

When all the school had gathered, Madame Rosa stood in the centre of the circle. 'I want each of you to come in turn into the circle. Miss Bluegrass will play and then you will begin. Each of you will perform the sequence from the Blue Moon Ballet as you have learned in lessons. Then you will await your cue, and each of you will perform your solo sequence. Now let us begin before you get too cold.'

Miss Bluegrass began to hum in a low voice and, after a few short notes, she began to sing out a haunting and delicate melody, signalling that it was time to dance.

Cassie soon forgot this was an important audition, and was wrapped up in enjoying the experience of dancing at night on the beach, listening to the soft call of the waves on the shore, and before she knew it, her name was being called.

She took up her place within the circle and glanced up at the night sky and at the shimmering moon. The moonlight made her feel powerful and the flickering flames helped keep her focus within the circle, the darkness outside it hiding all the usual distractions. It did not matter that her mind had panicked and forgotten the steps earlier, because as soon as she started to move, her body remembered all the hours of practice and instinctively she began the sequence. The dancing made her feel serene, and there was no space for panic or worry as she fluidly moved through the sweeping gestures, the pirouettes on the tips of her toes, the leaps through the moonlight . . . She stopped thinking about trying her best or feeling nervous, she just drank in the atmosphere and danced.

Whatever happens next, I feel that I have done my best, she thought, as she came to the end of the sequence. Her cheeks tingled with the cold, but her heart glowed as she waited for the cue to perform her original sequence. *I can make my mother proud of me.*

She had seen some of the complicated routines that the other sprites had performed before her, and a flicker of doubt passed through her as Mrs Sandskrit signalled for her to begin, but it was too late to change her mind now.

She took three long strides to the centre of the circle and stood in the spot where the moonbeams fell on to the sand. There she leaned forward and into a Sand

Stretch pose, standing unwavering in the moonlight for thirty long, unflinching seconds. All around she could hear other sand dancers fluttering and whispering, but Cassie remained still. Slowly she focused on what she felt was the key emotion of the ballet, *The ballet is all about looking back and regretting and wishing for a better life ahead.*

After a few moments more, Cassie was ready to begin dancing.

When everyone had performed, all the sand dancers walked silently back to the school where Miss Youngsand Snr made them drink a cup of warm sage tea before going back to bed.

No one had noticed the pair of wide green eyes, watching the whole event from a tuft of nearby grass.

Chapter Fourteen

'A sand dancer is never afraid
of facing the music and dancing.'
The Sands of Time

It wasn't until after lunch the following day that they learned the results of the audition. All the sprites wandered round as if they were dancing on sea shells.

'I would like the following sprites to stay behind,' Madame Rosa called out. 'Cassie, Calluna, Ella, Shell and Verbena. They will be the principal dancers of the Blue Moon Ballet. I thank the rest of you for all your hard work, and remind you that we each have a part to play in the ballet. No one part is greater than the whole of the performance. The chosen sprites have been selected because they have demonstrated the skills that are best suited for the dance sequence.'

Cassie turned to Shell. 'Did she call my name out?

Did she really call out my name? I thought it was the first one she said, but I might have been mistaken. I don't want to make a fool of myself.'

Shell hugged her friend. 'You're in! This time you made it!'

'Just don't let the group down,' Calluna said to her.

'Thanks for not putting the pressure on, Calluna,' Cassie said, smiling sweetly at her.

As the other sprites filed out, they made their way to the top table where Madame Rosa was waiting for them. Beside her was a pile of ancient-looking notebooks.

Madame Rosa smiled. 'From tomorrow, you will follow a different timetable from the rest of the class to prepare for the performance in one month's time. The next full moon, as I'm sure you're aware, will be a blue moon. It is a shame that Lexie was not able to dance for us, but the blue moon will not wait for anyone.' She handed each of them a booklet.

'These are the only remaining copies of the sequences of the Blue Moon Ballet. You will be expected to memorise the whole of the secret dune dance. Pay particular attention to the sequences leading up to the prima dune dancer's solo as they hold the clues for the replacement sequence that we will put together. You must learn the steps and then do your best to capture the essence of the dance – the dunes depend on it.'

Cassie was thrilled when it was her turn to be handed a booklet. She stroked its delicate purple felt cover.

'Take extra special care of these booklets. They are very precious. Under no circumstance must you lend them to anyone. Do you all understand?' Madame Rosa looked very serious. 'They are part of the series of secret dune dances that are known only to the sand dancers. They are vital to the survival of our home, the dunes, and so must be cared for accordingly. If the secrets of the dune dances fall into the hands of those who care not about the dunes, their power is diminished. Worse than that, it is thought that their powers can be manipulated in such a way that they could even cause damage to the dunes.'

All the sprites held on to their booklets even tighter when they heard this.

Madame Rosa turned to Cassie as they were leaving. 'You have been working hard and an improvement in your attitude and concentration has been noticed. I know that Marina would have been very proud of all the effort that you have put in. It was brave to trust your instincts at the audition. That is what a prima dune dancer does.'

Cassie floated all the way down the stairs to their next lesson – music. She had a feeling that any music she created today would be loud and booming.

The first thing Miss Bluegrass did was to make them all lie down on their tummies and close their eyes. 'Think beautiful thoughts. Only beautiful thoughts,' she commanded as she waved her arms.

Shell pulled an ugly face and Cassie struggled not to laugh.

'Now, listen to this sound and try to recreate it with your voices.' She played a few notes on her flute, which turned a delicate pink colour. 'The aim is to make your wings vibrate.'

'Strictly speaking they should only vibrate when we are dancing,' Calluna said.

Miss Bluegrass shook her head. 'Surely you haven't forgotten already what happened in the last lesson? Music can produce a similar healing effect on nature. Where I come from sand sprites are famed for their music. We all strive to get the purest sounds from our individual crystallophones. When this happens, our wings vibrate. Since I have been here, I have come to realise that we must combine music with dance. How much more harmony in the dunes we could create!'

Everyone tried even harder after that.

At the end of the session, Miss Bluegrass asked Cassie to stay behind and help tidy up. 'How are things going with you, Cassie? Did the audition go well? I was setting up for my music lesson over lunch and missed the announcement.'

'I'm going to be one of the principal dancers,' Cassie said, beaming.

Miss Bluegrass grinned back. 'I'm not surprised. You danced beautifully last night.'

Cassie felt herself blush. 'It will be a lot of hard work. I will have to concentrate really hard to learn the combination of steps.'

'How are you going to learn the sequences? I have heard that they are very complicated.'

'Madame Rosa has trusted us with the original booklets. They outline the secret combinations for the Blue Moon Ballet. We can only keep them until the performance though.'

'So that's how it works. Not so very different then from my dune where we have secret music booklets, although I'm sure no one would mind if I showed you one sometime, if you were interested.'

'That would be wonderful, if you were sure it was all right to do that,' Cassie replied.

Miss Bluegrass nodded. 'Actually, can you keep a secret?' She looked around her as Cassie nodded, and leaned in closer.

'Madame Rosa has asked me to compose a special piece of music for the ballet, incorporating all the harmonies of the dune. It would really help me if I could take a little peep at the booklet. I don't like to disturb Madame Rosa, and Mrs Sandskrit is not the most helpful sprite when it comes to supporting change.'

Cassie's fingers hovered over the cover of the book in her bag, Madame Rosa's warning echoing in her mind. *But*, she thought, *surely Madame Rosa hadn't meant teachers?*

Cassie pulled out the booklet and turned through the pages with Miss Bluegrass.

'All these diagrams are very confusing,' Miss Bluegrass frowned. 'I am not sure what all the patterns mean.'

'I could explain them to you,' Cassie said eagerly.

'That would be wonderful. Perhaps you could lend it to me for a little while?' Miss Bluegrass asked.

Cassie shook her head vigorously. 'Oh no. We are not allowed to do that. They have to be kept in our bags and looked after really well.'

'Sand dancers and their precious secrets,' Miss Bluegrass said with a laugh. 'Not to worry, I shall simply ask Madame Rosa for a copy some time.'

Cassie left the room quickly, feeling unsettled. A cold feeling was creeping up on her that was hard to figure out exactly, but even harder to ignore.

Chapter Fifteen

'Never underestimate the power of the tides.'
The Sands of Time

Over the next couple of weeks, Cassie spent many hours alone poring over the Blue Moon booklet. Each page was a series of complicated diagrams that marked out the dance sequence they were to perform as a group. After hours of study, they were slowly starting to make sense to her and, slowly, she began to be able to visualise the moves and then train her body to execute them. One day she had been so absorbed in imagining the dance that she hadn't noticed that she had caught her shrug on a nail. Half of it had become unravelled before she had realised.

All the rest of her time was taken up with rehearsing with the others. Her muscles ached and her head throbbed, but despite all that, Cassie had never felt more content about being a sand dancer. When Rubus returned with her mother, life would be perfect, she thought.

It was exciting to go off for private lessons with the rest of the principal performers but, while many sprites offered their congratulations, there were a few who started whispering or who shot her jealous looks when she passed by.

If they only knew how scared and nervous I am feeling deep down, she thought as she tried to shrug off their nasty looks. She wished she was more like Shell – she would simply put out her tongue and pull a face at the culprits.

She often closed her eyes and thought about the lantern show of her mother dancing – how easy she'd made the steps look! As if there was nothing more natural than twisting and turning oneself into all those shapes. What would her mother think of her dancing, she wondered.

It also made her think of Lysander and his account of Marina's dancing. With every spare moment given over to practising, there was no time to walk on the beach, and she'd seen no sign of him. Cassie reasoned that he must have jellycoptered off to another place. She liked to think that, wherever he was, he was dancing and maybe even planning a duet.

It seemed like the time would never pass and yet suddenly there were only two weeks to go to the performance.

Cassie's tummy rumbled as she got up from an after-noon sleep. She had become used to their new timetable now, and knew it was close to supper time. Cassie's tummy always seemed to know when it was time to eat. She was getting a bit fed up of the high energy health balls that they were given to eat at most meals these days, often washed down with large steaming bowls of sea bracken broth.

'Sea bracken broth, sea bracken broth,' Cassie sang out the words as she climbed down from her sleeping kutch. 'Sea bracken broth, I have so had enough of sea bracken broth.'

A voice replied, 'It would seem that I am back in the nick of time, then, with my box of sea cakes and blue-berry muffins.'

'LEXIE!' Cassie screamed in delight as she jumped down the rest of the steps and ran to hug her friend. 'When did you get back?' she asked, noting how thin her body felt beneath the hug.

'Only an hour ago. The dune bug seemed to take an age! First of all, Madame Rosa gave me a big talk about not overstretching myself, but then she gave me the best news: she told me I could start dancing straightaway! Isn't that wonderful? Miss Youngsand Snr made me swallow some green slime health tonic, and Mrs Sandskrit pinched my legs to check my muscle tone, and only then was I able to come to my kutch. I unpacked as quickly as I could and I came to find you and Shell.'

Cassie looked around. 'I wonder where Shell's got to? She might be dancing somewhere or sleeping – everything has been turned upside down for the Blue Moon Ballet.'

'She wasn't in her kutch or the practice room,' Lexie said. 'I was hoping we could get together and do the friendship promise before class. I can't wait to get started again.' Her eyes widened as she caught a glimpse inside Cassie's bag. 'Is that a Blue Moon booklet?'

Cassie's eyes sparkled. 'Yes, those of us who are taking part in the group dance have been trusted with the precious copies.'

'You got in!' Lexie exclaimed. 'How exciting! Well done! You are learning one of the secret dune dances. We are becoming real sand dancers!'

As they walked towards the dining hall, Lexie asked, 'Why's everyone wearing what looks like giant samphire buns in their hair?'

'Shell started it. I told you about it in the letter, but since then the fashion has spread throughout the school. My hair is too fine to wear them. Just wait till you see Miss Bluegrass's hair. She wears a headdress that has bells and flutes in it and you can actually hear her before you see her! She is an amazing teacher. I have begun to write songs. Miss Bluegrass thinks I show promise.'

'That's wonderful. I'd love to hear them later.' Lexie linked arms with her friend as they entered the dining hall, where Shell whooped with joy to see her. Madame

Rosa walked over to them as they were about to take their seats.

'It looks like you are settling back in, Alexsandra. I have spoken with Mrs Sandskrit and we are both agreed that you will join the training with the principal dancers in the ballet. Cassie, you can show her what we have learned so far. It will do you good to show someone else the steps – it's a certain way to improve one's own technique. Cassie will share her copy of the booklet with you. Let's hope you can get up to speed in a couple of weeks, and if you are capable of performing, then you will.'

Lexie curtseyed, blushing. 'Thank you so much, Madame Rosa. It is a dream of mine to dance in the Blue Moon Ballet.'

All the sprites around them exchanged glances. Lexie was being offered a part in the ballet as a principal dancer without having to audition.

'Is that quite fair, Madame? I mean the auditions have taken place,' Calluna asked sourly.

Madame Rosa looked faintly surprised. 'I hope you are not questioning my judgement, Calluna. That would be extremely disrespectful,' she said, and left them to their sea bracken broth.

'They have probably taken pity on me because I've missed so much time,' Lexie said to Shell and Cassie, as they walked to the music room together after supper.

'Pity and Mrs Sandskrit do not go together,' Shell snorted.

'It's because you are the best sand dancer,' Cassie said. She found that she could admit this now, without feeling jealous of Lexie.

'It is not going to help Calluna and I to become friends,' Lexie whispered. 'Did you see the look she gave me? It would melt the moon! Anyway, tell me more about these music lessons.'

'They are the complete opposite from Mrs Sandskrit's and Madame Rosa's classes, where you know how you are expected to behave – you never know what is going to happen!' Cassie paused. 'It will be interesting to see what you think of Miss Bluegrass.'

Cassie and Shell explained their different views of Miss Bluegrass to Lexie – and managed not to argue!

Miss Bluegrass was waiting for them at the door of the music room. 'So this is Alexsandra Seacouch. I have heard so much about you. I hope you are feeling better. Welcome to the music class.'

Lexie smiled at her. 'I am so pleased to meet you. I have never had a music lesson before.'

'Perfect! Then you will have no fixed ideas!' Miss Bluegrass said as she led them in. She handed everyone a glass of water.

'I want you to take a sip and gargle it in the back of your throat and make a noise like so.' She made a bubbling sound in her voice. It was fun, but some of the sand sprites swallowed a lot of water or got attacks of the giggles before they could make any sound.

'Right, now we are all relaxed, let's hear your compositions,' Miss Bluegrass said.

Everyone settled down around the crystallophone to listen to the songs they had composed to fit the music Miss Bluegrass had played for them previously.

When it was her turn, Cassie swallowed. 'My composition is called *"Betrayer Moon"*, because that is sometimes another name for a blue moon.' The words had come to her one evening almost without her thinking about them.

'Was I wrong to trust you?
To dance with you in the dunes?
Have I whispered all my secrets
to a pale betrayer moon?'

Miss Bluegrass nodded. 'Betrayal is such a complicated emotion.'

'Why is that?' Lexie asked.

Miss Bluegrass's voice wavered. 'Sometimes loyalties can be divided and difficult choices have to be made. More often than not, family blood wins through.'

For the first time in days, Cassie thought about her mother. *Where was she? Would she ever return to Dreamy Dune?*

133

Chapter Sixteen

'A sand dancer should always hope for the best,
but be prepared for the worst.'
The Sands of Time

It was great to have Lexie back, but it was strange too. Shell and Cassie had got used to functioning as a pair and they found they kept forgetting to include Lexie. Cassie and Shell lost count of the number of times they had to stick up for Lexie when jealous sprites made comments about her 'just walking in and getting a main part'.

'And I thought sand dancing was all about preserving the dunes by performing the secret steps. I didn't think mean spritedness came into it,' Shell rounded on them. No one could argue with that.

For her part, Lexie proved the point by quickly mastering the dance steps for the sequence, even though she found it hard to adjust to the nocturnal timetable.

The Blue Moon Ballet was getting very close. After class one day, Cassie headed up to her kutch to study the Blue Moon booklet yet again. As she passed Ella's kutch, she heard a strange sound. She poked her head around the curtain and saw Ella, sitting on the floor with her head resting on her knees, crying.

'Ella, whatever is wrong?' asked Cassie softly.

Ella looked up in tears. 'Oh, Cassie, something terrible has happened.'

Cassie kneeled down and put an arm around Ella. 'Whatever it is, we'll find a way to put it right. But what has happened?'

'I . . . I've lost my Blue Moon booklet! I definitely had it two days ago, but I only noticed it was missing today. I know all the moves, of course, but then I wanted to check a couple of them and, when I looked in my bag, it wasn't there. What am I going to do? I've let everyone down.'

Cassie offered her a handkerchief and Ella began to dab her eyes.

'Come on,' said Cassie, pulling Ella up by the hand. 'Let's go and look for it now. I'm sure it will only be a case of retracing your dance steps.'

Cassie and Ella spent half the night tiptoeing around the school, but they found nothing.

'We'll have to let Madame Rosa know that a booklet has been misplaced,' Cassie said.

'No, not yet,' Ella pleaded. 'I'm sure I can find it. Just

give me another day.'

Cassie reluctantly agreed. If the book didn't turn up by the next afternoon, then she would ask Shell and Lexie for help.

Lexie had been so busy catching up with the principal dancers she had had hardly any time to talk to Cassie and Shell. The next afternoon they arranged to meet in the Secrets Cupboard. No one could sleep because there was now only one day left before the night of the dress rehearsal.

'You were not kidding when you said it had changed in here,' Lexie whistled when she saw how clean the cupboard was. 'Where have all the old costumes gone?'

'Some of them are still in this wicker basket and Miss Youngsand Snr moved some to the sewing room. This basket used to be full of velvet curtains, but they are now being used to soundproof the music room.' Cassie told her all about how they put up the curtains in Miss Bluegrass's room.

'Miss Bluegrass still believes that it was Mrs Sandskrit's idea,' Cassie chuckled, 'but at least they have been getting along better since then.'

Lexie dangled her long legs over the side of the wicker basket. 'It is amazing how quickly my body is getting used to all this dancing again. Your Aunt Euphorbia was a great help showing me how to practise when I was recovering.'

Cassie looked shocked. 'Slippery sea slugs! That is a surprise! She hates dancing! Surely I told you how she came bursting into the audition in a terrible rage and forbade me to dance.'

Lexie giggled. 'Oh yes – I remember you and Shell telling me! But, I have come up with a theory about why she hates dancing so much. I think you only really hate the things that you have once loved. Your aunt must have really loved dancing at one time.'

'Only you could come up with such an outrageous theory,' Cassie said. But suddenly she remembered that strange image that had got mixed up with the Blue Moon Ballet. There had been something familiar about the serious expression on the girl's face. Yes! She realised who the dancer reminded her of – Aunt Euphorbia. 'Do you think it's possible?' she asked Lexie, once she had told her the story.

'It's certainly possible,' Lexie replied. 'Your poor aunt – if it was her. My heart would break if I couldn't dance any more. Hating it would be the easiest option.' She hunched her shoulders and drew her knees tightly to her chest. 'I am finding it hard to cope with all the snide comments at the moment. I wish that I hadn't been offered a part. I can almost understand why the others feel peeved – I mean I did just walk into a leading role.'

'You were born to be a great dancer, Lexie. And that also means that you were born to help the dunes when they are in most danger. True sand dancers know this.

Nothing else matters.'

'Thank you, Cassie. It means a lot to me to have you and Shell as my friends. I know it hasn't been easy since I came back. I feel a bit out of step with everyone.'

At that moment the door of the Secrets Cupboard was flung open and Shell burst in. She was hot and breathless and she clutched at Cassie's arm.

'What is it?' Cassie asked, as Shell collapsed on to the edge of the wicker basket.

She held her side and gasped, 'Just let me catch my breath.' She took a few deep breaths and sat up straight. 'I'm all right now. I've just raced back from the beach.' Shell lowered her voice. 'We have some definite proof that Miss Bluegrass is a spy! I can hardly believe it myself, but I have just seen Miss Bluegrass hand over a Blue Moon booklet to Lysander.'

'Are you absolutely sure?' Cassie's eyes widened with shock.

'I was going for a walk to clear my head. It was then that I saw them.' Shell's blue eyes flashed with anger.

'There might be a perfectly reasonable explanation,' Lexie said. 'You can't be absolutely sure what you saw.'

'Oh, Lexie, I really hope that you are right, because we are supposed to guard the secrets of the dune dances with our lives. The Prince of Tides could use this as evidence of our weakness and seize control. If he ever got to learn the dances in the correct sequence, he might be able to unlock the power of the dunes.'

'What exactly did you see?' Cassie asked.

'I crouched low in the grass, because they kept constantly looking around to see if they were being watched. I saw Miss Bluegrass. She was wearing a large headscarf, probably to muffle the noise of her hair, and I saw her hand over a Blue Moon booklet to Lysander – I recognised the purple cover with a picture of a blue moon on it. How did she get a copy?'

Cassie bit on her lip. 'Ella's booklet has gone missing,' she said quietly.

'What!' Shell and Lexie said together.

'Ella was in a dreadful state yesterday. She made me promise not to tell anyone while she kept looking for it. She was so upset. We thought it had just been lost – not stolen . . . But perhaps Miss Bluegrass did just find it.'

The look on Shell's face told them she did not think this was true.

'There must be another explanation. It is too awful to imagine that she really has betrayed us,' said Cassie, jumping up. 'I'll go back to the beach, find Lysander and demand to know what is going on. If he has it, I will get that booklet back.'

Cassie rushed out of the ground-floor peephole, and down to the beach, but the beach was empty.

Cassie thought hard as she raced back to the school. She was pretty certain that Lysander had got hold of Shell's page of the Blue Moon Ballet steps, because Ella had seen him dancing on the beach and she had seen

Miss Bluegrass with the sheet. He had been sneaking about the school ever since term started – he had been the source of the scent of wild thyme. Why would Miss Bluegrass give a secret Blue Moon booklet with the complete ballet steps to a surf boy? But Lysander was no ordinary surf boy – he could interpret their dances really quickly. Had he tricked her into handing it over, somehow? The words of her song suddenly came into her head.

'Was I wrong to trust you?
To dance with you in the dunes?
Have I whispered all my secrets
to a pale betrayer moon?'

She repeated them over and over again, as she returned to the Secrets Cupboard.

'There was no sign of anyone on the beach,' Cassie reported.

'I knew there would be no trace of them. He is probably long gone with the booklet. I bet the Prince of Tides will pay him well for it,' Shell said bitterly.

'Tell me about Lysander,' Lexie suggested, after a moment's silence.

'He seemed a maddeningly self-confident surf boy,' said Shell.

'But he does love dancing,' said Cassie. 'He will do anything to learn how to dance. He can't help himself. I think he's been sneaking into Sandringham to watch the classes, and I bet he was watching the auditions on the beach. And . . . I think he took your sequence page, Shell. There is something wild and unpredictable about him.'

'The slimy sand worm!' Shell cried, and then paused. 'I bet he used his charm on Miss Bluegrass to trick her into handing over the booklet and the page. Miss Bluegrass is the weakest link in the school and the obvious way for him to get hold of a booklet,' Shell continued, as she paced the room.

'It would help,' said Lexie, 'if we knew exactly what Miss Bluegrass was doing on the beach and how she knows Lysander. I wonder if we should tell Madame Rosa. If Lysander is just keen on dancing, that is all right. But if he is snooping around for other purposes . . .'

'Lysander may well be working for the Prince of Tides,' said Shell. 'But there's no way he'd leave before the performance of the Blue Moon Ballet – if he is going to interpret the moves he'd want to see it, and he'd never get back in time if he left today.'

'So for the moment we keep an eye on Miss Bluegrass, and see if we can find Lysander,' said Cassie.

'Yes,' agreed Shell. 'We need to be certain there's a real problem before we alert anyone else.'

Chapter Seventeen

*'Decorum and a sense of balance are what makes
the sand dancer stand out from the crowd.'*
The Sands of Time

'A sand dancer should never look flustered. She must
remain calm and collected and never allow any tension
to show on her face,' Miss Youngsand Snr told the etiquette class the next morning. She'd clearly had enough
of all the fidgeting throughout her lesson, but no one
could keep still. It was the dress rehearsal that evening.

'Now, I want each of you to balance your exercises
book on your head and walk around the edge of the
pool, maintaining an upright and balanced posture. I
will demonstrate.'

All the sand dancers watched in awe as Miss
Youngsand Snr placed the exercises book on the top of
her pile of braids and steadily made her way towards the

side of the pool. She stretched out and pointed one of her slippers very close to the water's edge. Then she delicately reached out the other foot, turned round to everyone, and indicated they should do the same.

They were all concentrating hard – one slip could mean a soggy exercises book – when Ella came rushing up to the pool.

'Sorry I am late.' She bowed low; her hair was crumpled and bent out of shape.

Miss Youngsand Snr wobbled and leaned precariously towards the pool. At the last moment, she arched her back, and held her balance.

'Ella, I am surprised at you,' she exclaimed. 'Not only have you arrived late and tested my sense of balance to the maximum, but you are in a state of disarray. Please sort yourself out!'

'Sorry.' Ella dropped her head as she patted her hair and attempted to smooth her creased skirt. She turned, her lips trembling and whispered to Cassie, 'I'd better start packing. I've looked everywhere now and I still can't find the booklet. It was my last chance – we have to hand them in tonight. How could I have been so careless? My life is ruined!'

'Try not to worry. Your friends will stick by you,' Cassie replied.

Ella looked up hopefully at Cassie. 'I have been sick with worry and shame. I just can't think what I've done with it. I must have taken it out without thinking or left it in my sleeping kutch.'

'I'm not promising anything, but I think I have a lead. I will try my very best to see it is returned to you before we have to hand them in.' Cassie tried to make her voice sound more confident than she felt.

Ella gave a sigh of relief. 'If anyone can get me out of this mess, I'm sure you can, Cassie.'

After etiquette class, everyone was ordered to go down to the beach to help prepare the stage for the dress rehearsal.

Miss Youngsand Jnr held up a large sketch. 'As you know the stage is in the shape of a spiral like the inside of a sea shell. There are just a few final pieces of shell to add.'

Miss Youngsand Snr stood on a small box, to make herself as tall as her sister, and said, 'Please make sure you bend your legs. I don't want any accidents or torn back muscles.'

'Mrs Sandskrit said that I have to rest, so please may I be excused.' Lexie curtseyed, ignoring the mean looks and mimicking from some of the others.

'Who does she think she is, a prima dune dancer?' Cassie heard someone say.

'This is a good chance for me to do some spying on Miss Bluegrass while everyone else is here,' Lexie whispered to Shell and Cassie. 'If I need help, I will hang my scarf from Cassie's balcony.'

The sand sprites tied their scarves over their heads to protect themselves from the sun and the winds. After an hour of hard slog, moving beams, tying shells together and smoothing the sand, Miss Youngsand Snr told them to do some stretching exercises.

'Cassie,' Calluna said suddenly, 'I think you had better go and sort out your kutch. Some of your clothes are in danger of flying out of the peephole.'

Cassie looked up. A red scarf was fluttering in the sea breeze from her balcony.

'Go and sort it out, at once,' Miss Youngsand Snr ordered, but Cassie was already running back towards the school.

She found Lexie waiting for her at the main entrance.

'Miss Bluegrass has just let Lysander in through a ground-floor peephole,' she said breathlessly.

Cassie thought for a moment, then said resolutely, 'Lexie, you should go back to the beach, to the other sprites. This is partly my fault and I should deal with it.'

Lexie paused, then nodded and left.

Cassie tiptoed slowly down the large staircase. Every sound was magnified in the silence and she tried to remember which steps creaked. As she reached the bottom of the staircase, she took three long deep breaths and rested her hand on her heart to try and calm it down. It was beating far too fast and noisily.

The sound of footsteps at the far end of the corridor made her freeze and tiptoe closer to the edge of the wall, trying to melt into the shadows.

'I hope it made some sense to you,' Miss Bluegrass was saying.

'Can't I keep it a while longer? I am just beginning to understand the moves. It is a tremendous ballet,' Lysander's voice pleaded. 'It's far too complicated to copy out. And I don't understand everything yet.'

'No. I must have it back. Mrs Sandskrit will be collecting them in soon and suspicions will be aroused if a Blue Moon booklet goes missing. Besides, I don't want Ella to get into any trouble. The poor child is already nearly melting with fear.'

'I have put too much pressure on you already – I'm sorry. It's just that it's my dream – I have come too far to be disappointed now. I know I can become a great sand dancer if only I could get the chance.' He held out the booklet to Miss Bluegrass.

Cassie stepped forward and snatched it from a surprised-looking Lysander. 'Ella has been tormented. What do you think you're doing? You've caused Ella so much pain!'

'I thought all the sand dancers were outside preparing for the dress rehearsal,' Miss Bluegrass exclaimed, looking shocked.

But Lysander looked at Cassie seriously and answered her question. 'You must forgive me, Cassie, for having been so selfish. I never thought of Ella getting into trouble. But I can explain . . .'

He moved towards Cassie, who took a step back, holding tightly on to the booklet.

Lysander continued. 'I have always loved dancing and, as you know, that is not very usual for a surf boy. I especially wanted to learn at the Sandringham Dance School so, when my mother received the invitation from Madame Rosa, I begged her to let me come along too. I have been learning all I can and waiting for a chance to show my dancing skills to Madame Rosa.'

So Miss Bluegrass was Lysander's mother! Somehow Cassie felt relieved that they were related.

'Do you think she will let me join the school?' Lysander asked.

Cassie crossed her arms. 'Madame Rosa is fair-minded so she may give you a chance. But are *you* worthy after stealing a Blue Moon booklet? At Sandringham, you are judged both on your dancing ability and your good character and I can only honestly vouch for one of those things.' She paused. 'It's such a relief that you have explained everything though. For a moment there you had us convinced that you were spies carrying information to the Prince of Tides.'

Cassie felt so relieved that she practically flew off to tell Shell and Lexie what had happened.

Chapter Eighteen

*'The moon and the tide are like an argumentative sister
and brother who pull together in troubled times.'*
The Sands of Time

After their afternoon nap, Cassie found Ella crouching
down by the side of the stage, chewing on her nails.

'You need to get changed, and practise wearing your
headdress – the dress rehearsal will begin soon. We have
to go and hand in our Blue Moon booklets too, so you'll
need this.' She pushed something into Ella's hands.

'My Blue Moon booklet! Where did you find it? Oh,
Cassie, I don't care. All that matters is that you've got it
back. Thank you so much!' The fear and anxiety drained
from Ella's face.

'It is all right. Now we must all focus on tonight's
performance,' Cassie replied.

Cassie took three large deep breaths and tried to

empty her mind of everything but the dance. She went through all the steps in her mind and pictured the scene. Then she did her warm-up stretches and completed a quick walk-through of the steps with the other dancers out on the stage.

The teachers were fussing too. Miss Youngsand Snr made some last-minute alterations to the costumes, and Miss Youngsand Jnr changed the position of the shell pathways on the stage, ordering all the torches to be removed, then put back in exactly the same place a few minutes later. Mrs Sandskrit wanted to hear Miss Bluegrass's music performed in three different ways.

When the dancers were all ready, Mrs Sandskrit came and inspected them, and made everyone retie their dancing slippers again.

'This is the dress rehearsal. I want you to concentrate on your technique and getting the moves as perfect as you can. You should be able to do them almost without thinking now. Once we add the atmosphere of the full blue moon, everything should come together. I'm sure I don't need to tell you just how important this is. We only get one chance to perform the ballet tomorrow night, so let's endeavour to be the best we can.'

All the sand dancers nodded.

Mrs Sandskrit smiled. 'Let the dance begin.'

It was a windy night and the flames from the torches bent and switched direction; as well as remembering their steps, the dancers had to avoid getting too close to them.

Cassie thought about what Mrs Sandskrit had told them about working with nature, using the breeze and the moonlight, to help communicate the spirit of dance.

The music from Miss Bluegrass's crystallophone was very haunting and did help them move more gracefully. It seemed to seep into their bodies like smoke and change the way they felt, evoking memories long buried.

The dancers understood that there would be no interruptions in the dress rehearsal. If anything went wrong, they were to continue and make the best of it – just as if it were the night of the performance. And some things did go wrong. A few of the dancers hesitated and lost their rhythm, and a couple of headdresses fell off during a run of Dart and Turns. But the power of the dance was such that they overcame these problems and danced on. The Blue Moon Ballet was finally coming together.

But then a sudden gust of wind caught the flames and, for a few seconds, they pointed in completely the opposite direction. In that moment, they lit up the edge of a dune and fell like a spotlight on the surf boy who was dancing the steps along with the dancers, his moves as perfect as theirs. He did not notice the lights on him. With gasps of amazement, everyone began to watch him and the ballet came to an abrupt halt.

Miss Bluegrass stopped playing and turned to look. 'Lysander! No! Stop – you are spoiling the dress rehearsal. We need to practise!' she shouted in a loud and angry voice and then she collapsed, overcome by shock.

Lysander froze, horrified, as he realised everyone could see. As if on cue, the wind changed direction again and he was lost in the dark shadows of the dune. A few moments later, he reappeared beside his mother and scooped her up in his arms.

'What is the meaning of this intrusion? Who are you and why are you trying to ruin the ballet?' Madame Rosa angrily demanded.

'How do you know these steps?' asked Mrs Sandskrit as she crossed the stage.

'Mother,' Lysander said softly, and began to rub her hands.

Miss Bluegrass opened her eyes and tried to smile. 'I'll be fine. Give me a moment to gather myself. We have to tell them the whole truth, Lysander. No matter what the consequence,' she said in a weak voice.

'I think we'd better go back to the school,' said Madame Rosa in a cold voice. 'There is obviously much that you need to tell me.'

Cassie watched them, relieved that their secret was now out in the open.

Chapter Nineteen

*'A prima dune dancer's first priority
is to protect and honour the dunes.'
The Sands of Time*

Cassie felt as though there was a miniature sand factory inside her head, sifting and pounding away at the jumble of her thoughts and feelings.

Madame Rosa had demanded absolute silence as she sent the sand dancers straight to their beds. Cassie splashed some cold water on her face and carefully got out of her beautiful blue moon costume. The silver sparkles shone in the moonlight and she carefully smoothed out all the strands in the skirt.

She tried to rest her head on the pillow, but couldn't find a space to get comfortable, and all the time the beat kept on pounding in her head and the words of her song about the betrayer moon danced on her nerves.

She took a large sip of water, but her throat still felt like dry grass.

'Must sleep. Big day tomorrow,' Cassie told herself as she squeezed her eyes shut, but she couldn't help worrying. Sleep was the most important thing she had to do at that moment, but every time she was close to it, the beating would hammer her awake again.

She drifted in and out of consciousness. At one point she dreamed that someone was climbing up the ladder to her balcony.

'Cassie,' said a voice. 'I'm back.' It sounded like Rubus.

Cassie could not bear this dream again. She was tired of dreaming about the return of her mother or Rubus. She did not have time to deal with the feelings of disappointment that would come when she woke up.

'Go away! I am tired of dreaming about your return and you never come and my head is hurting me. Go away!' she screamed deliriously.

Then she dreamed that something cold and comforting seeped into the side of her face and she felt a hand stroke her hair.

The voice whispered, 'You will be fine, Cassie.'

'My head hurts. It's pounding.'

'It's a tension headache. I used to get them all the time before a big ballet. Drink this.'

Cassie imagined a shell goblet held to her lips and she drank the cooling liquid.

'Now sleep and you will wake refreshed.'

153

After this, Cassie fell into a deep sleep.

She woke up feeling completely rested. The air around her seemed to smell of roses and sea kelp – her mother's favourite perfume. Cassie gulped down three bowls of sea bracken soup for breakfast. She was just deciding whether to have another slice of laver bread when Shell and Lexie joined her.

'What a night!' she said. 'I had so many restless dreams, but this morning I feel ready for anything!'

Just then Ella raced in. 'Madame Rosa wants to see you in the dance studio at once,' she said to Cassie. 'I have never seen her looking so fierce and angry.'

'Maybe I'm not quite ready for *anything*,' Cassie said, frowning.

On her way to the studio, Cassie bumped into Thassalinus carrying a basket of shells. 'Good to have a surf boy about the place again, isn't it?' he said.

'Not if they cause so much trouble,' she snapped back at him.

Madame Rosa was in the studio, with Mrs Sandskrit, Lysander and Miss Bluegrass. Cassie could feel the tension crackling in the air.

'Cassie, it seems you have met Lysander before,' Madame Rosa said. 'And you know that Miss Bluegrass is his mother. Miss Bluegrass has admitted to showing Lysander some material on the Blue Moon Ballet, and Lysander has confessed to sneaking around the school and watching us practise. But it seems that you have danced in front of him – indeed, with him – and may also have shown him our secret dance steps. Surely you know how serious that is?'

Cassie looked down at the floor in misery. 'Lysander is such a talented dancer and I just found myself dancing with him. I deeply regret if I have caused any harm.'

Madame Rosa's hard expression seemed to soften. 'Cassie, Miss Bluegrass has something to tell you,' she said.

Miss Bluegrass sobbed. 'Oh, Cassie! I did originally come to this school as a spy for the Prince of Tides. Lysander was to be my messenger. But he has always loved dancing, and by being here he has grown even more obsessed.'

Cassie's toes started to tingle with rage and she yelled, 'So Shell was right all along! I trusted you and I defended you. How could you? You were only nice to me because you thought you'd then be able to get information from me. You are loathesome!'

Miss Bluegrass blew her nose loudly and gulped back her tears. 'The Prince had convinced me that sand dancers were not worthy of their powers. But it wasn't long before I knew that I could never betray you all. I have fallen in love with this place and everyone in it . . .' She gave a small smile. '. . . Even Mrs Sandskrit whom I respect and admire. I am in awe of your sense of dedication and loyalty. I can feel the power of your dancing as a force for good. Instead of betraying you, I have done my best to make the Blue Moon Ballet wonderful – you know I have.'

Lysander put his arm around his mother as he spoke. 'I was supposed to pass on everything that my mother found out, and I haven't done that. We both decided that we wouldn't cooperate with the Prince. It is true that my mother showed me pages from the Blue Moon Ballet booklet. I studied them because I love dance, not because I was going to betray the sand dancers. I made my mind up about that when I danced with Cassie.'

'It seems that my "friend" who suggested Miss Bluegrass to me did not have the noble intentions that I had thought. The truth of their words is what we have to decide now, Cassie,' said Madame Rosa. 'And you have an important part to play. We only caught a glimpse of Lysander dancing on the sand. We want to see the dune duet that we have been told about. You can tell a lot about a sprite's character when you watch them dance.'

Cassie felt her body fill up with ice crystals. She had been so wrong to dance with Lysander and now she was going to have to dance with him again – in front of Madame Rosa and Mrs Sandskrit.

Perhaps I should refuse, she thought. *Whatever I do, Madame Rosa will never trust me again.*

Lysander stepped towards Cassie. 'Dancing is the only decent thing I can do with my life. You've got to help me. We have to trust each other absolutely to do the dune duet. Will you give me a second chance and trust me?'

Cassie nodded slowly. 'When we are dancing, I trust

you completely. It is the rest of the time that I am not sure.'

And so they began.

At first they were awkward together. Cassie did not feel comfortable being watched and it felt different dancing in the practice room and not on the beach. But, after a minute, she began to adjust and to forget about the audience. It was only when Lysander lifted her that she became aware again of Madame Rosa and Mrs Sandskrit watching her, an unreadable look on their faces. She wavered slightly, but Lysander held on to her tightly, his will and determination keeping her moving.

After the duet was finished, nobody spoke for a long time. As Cassie and Lysander stood together, she could feel his heart beating hard, but he stood up strong and tall.

'I thank you for granting me the opportunity of dancing before you,' Lysander said suddenly and, bowing graciously, he left the room.

Cassie suddenly felt cold. What was going to happen next? Was she going to be asked to leave Sandringham for having danced secretly with a surf boy? No, worse – a spy?

Madame Rosa and Mrs Sandskrit exchanged glances.

'Thank you for your help, Cassie. You may go and rest now. You will still dance tonight – it is too late to change the principal dancers. We need some time to decide calmly what our next move is and to consult with Sandrine. We will be able to tell tonight whether our secrets have been passed on. If the dunes react to the Blue Moon Ballet, then we will know that the magic has not been broken.'

Cassie went to her kutch, exhausted. She lay still on her bed, afraid to think of anything beyond that night's performance.

Chapter Twenty

*'Be silent and still and listen to the sounds of the shell,
for they whisper the secrets of the sea.'*
The Sands of Time

Despite everything that had happened, Cassie was bursting with energy when she awoke. The night of the Blue Moon Ballet had come at last!

She realised that, in spite of everything, she did believe Miss Bluegrass and Lysander when they said they hadn't passed on the secret dance steps. She felt certain that the strength of the Blue Moon Ballet would be felt tonight. If this was going to be her last chance to dance before being sent home in disgrace, she was going to dance with all her heart.

Cassie put on her practice dress and went out on to the balcony for a peek at the stage. From where she was standing, she could clearly see the spiral outline of the shell path on the sand. The sea formed a dark blue back-drop and the dunes were the sides of the stage. To crown it all, there was a large pale blue moon in the sky.

Thassalinus was busy lighting the torches and the audience was already beginning to gather.

A wave of excitement crashed in her stomach, and she climbed down the ladder to join the others. As she was walking along the corridor, an arm reached out and grabbed her. She gasped and turned round.

'Rubus, is it really you?' Cassie asked.

'A few more muscles from working on a sand galleon, but it is still the same old me,' Rubus smiled. 'I haven't got much time. In fact, I shouldn't have left the beach, but I couldn't wait to see you and find out how you were.'

Cassie looked at Rubus and suddenly felt awkward and shy.

'I am fine. We have all been working like mad to prepare for the Blue Moon Ballet. But, tell me – oh, please tell me. What about you – the journey, and . . .?'

Cassie saw that there was an added firmness to his jaw and some shadows under his eyes. She sensed that something had changed between them.

'It was harder than you could ever imagine. There were some amazing sights, but there were also some really scary moments. The world is such a large place, full of kindness and cruelty in equal measures.' His eyes darted around. 'The news is good, Cassie. We found what we were looking for and —'

'There you are, Cassie. What are you doing lurking in the dark corridor? I have been searching for you everywhere.' Lysander ran up to her. 'Oh, I didn't realise you had company.' He bowed. 'You are Rubus, I presume.'

'And you are?' Rubus gave him a menacing look.

'This is Lysander. The son of the visiting music teacher,' Cassie said quickly, keen to get rid of him and desperate to hear the news of her mother.

'I just came to wish you luck, and thank you. I am still waiting to hear what is to happen to me from Madame Rosa. Tonight I am confident that the sand dancers will make the dunes sing.' He bowed and then he left.

'What was that all about?' Rubus asked.

'It's a long story and I really have to go and get ready for the performance, but, please, quickly, tell me about my mother.'

'She is safe and well,' Rubus reassured her. 'And not far from here. You will meet her soon. Now go, quickly. We will talk properly after the performance.'

Before Cassie could say anything else or ask more about her mother, he had melted back into the darkness and she could hear Shell calling out for her.

The ballet was about to begin.

161

Chapter Twenty-one

*'Happiness is often to be found
between a rock and a hard place.'*
The Sands of Time

'You're cutting it a bit fine,' Lexie said as she helped Cassie into her dress in the changing rooms. Lexie was dying to know what had happened, but there was no time. Cassie wanted to tell her about Rubus, but another sprite came in to put on her make-up and she had to be still while the blue lipstick was applied and the pale white powder was dusted on to her face.

'Stop frowning, Cassie, or the powder will settle in the lines and you'll look awful,' Lexie said, and then she squeezed her friend's arm. 'You are going to be fine, Cassie. You have worked so hard.'

Cassie gulped back a tear. 'I don't know if I can do this. Now that I am here, I don't feel ready.'

'I will not accept such a negative attitude,' a voice boomed out.

Cassie and Lexie turned round to see Calluna standing there. She walked towards them. She was already wearing her magnificent blue moon headdress and in her full make-up.

'This is no time for a crisis of confidence, Cassandra Marramgrass. We are all depending on you. If you waver, then it will affect the rest of us. Now stand up and start to stretch and warm up!'

Cassie and Lexie looked at each other, surprised that any form of encouragement should come from Calluna. Ella, Shell and Verbena joined them, made-up and ready in their costumes.

'Sand dancers never give up – even when things look impossible, we keep trying!' Calluna continued.

'Thank you, Calluna, you have firmed up my pre-show wobble.' Cassie smiled at the senior sand dancer who, to Cassie's amazement, returned the smile.

They all linked arms together and walked down to the stage.

As they waited in the dunes at the side of the stage, Cassie tried to clear her mind and it took her a few minutes to get her focus on the dance. She did not dare look out into the audience, but instead she stared up. The clouds had lifted, leaving the full moon clear in the sky.

'It's amazing, isn't it?' Ella stood by her. 'I have never seen a blue moon before.'

'It's shining just for us. The perfect backdrop for our ballet,' Lexie whispered.

Before they took their places, Miss Youngsand Snr gave them all a hot rosehip cordial to sip. 'The night is cold and this will give you energy. Sandrine has just arrived, so we will be starting soon,' she said.

Miss Bluegrass arrived wearing a blue shimmering dress. She tried to catch Cassie's eyes, but Cassie could not bring herself to look at her quite yet. She still felt betrayed and hurt by her and was afraid she would begin a massive Rage Stomp when she needed to stay calm to perform the dance.

The audience was beginning to quieten, and Madame Rosa addressed the dancers. 'If all goes well tonight the performance of the Blue Moon Ballet will be a very powerful experience and I have to warn you to be prepared for strange happenings as you dance. The wind may appear stronger on your face or the sands may shift beneath your feet. You may hear some noises or feel vibrations. You must keep on dancing. This is your first duty as sand dancers. You must keep on dancing! If we are very lucky the dunes will answer us.' Madame Rosa's eyes flashed.

Mrs Sandskrit clapped her hands. 'To your places, dancers! If you remember that the dance begins and ends in your heart and stay true to yourselves, you will not go wrong.'

The sand dancers followed the shell path to their places.

As Cassie reached her position on the stage, her heart was pounding with fear and excitement. She glanced into the crowd and thought she caught a glimpse of Rubus, but when she looked again he had gone.

Everyone fell silent as the twelve notes of the crystallophone rang out. It was time for the ballet to start.

Chapter Twenty-two

'The dance begins and ends in your heart.'
The Sands of Time

The beams of moonlight fell across the stage as the ballet began. Cassie and her friends had never worked so hard. When Cassie began to get tired, a look from Calluna, a smile from Lexie and a wink from Shell kept her dancing.

When the moment came for their group dance, the dancers squeezed hands as they formed a circle. They performed the steps that had once seemed so difficult, so strange to them, but now, on the stage, beneath the blue moon, felt so natural.

Lexie, who was partnering Cassie, danced as if she had been practising the steps for years instead of days. Each move she made inspired Cassie.

A low haunting sound began to seep into the night air. The sound built up in intensity until it seemed the ground was gently vibrating. The air became still and hot and then from out of nowhere a series of cool breezes began to blow. The dunes were reacting to the dancing. Cassie trembled when she realised what was happening. The Blue Moon Ballet had retained its powers!

The principal dancers then fanned out and took their places to wait through Miss Bluegrass's solo of the beautiful crystallophone music, where the prima dune dancer would have once danced the solo.

The notes from the crystallophone blended with the vibrations from the dunes. Gradually they began to build up to a climax and then the sounds died away.

All was still and silent. Cassie took a breath. She could feel her heart fluttering in her ribcage. The stage was empty apart from the pale moonbeams.

Then the music began – and a dancer leaped from a dune and into the centre circle of the stage. She was dressed in a series of long flowing scarves of different shades of blue that swept around her body and face.

A murmur went round the audience as the dancer began to dance. It took Cassie's breath away to watch. The dancer and the moon performed a perfect dance exactly as she had seen it in the lantern show.

At one point, the dancer passed close to where Cassie was standing, and one of the scarves touched her. A wave of rose and sea kelp perfume confirmed what Cassie knew in her heart.

As the dancer floated around the stage, she rose on

her toes and turned her arms and performed one, two, three jumps and leg crosses. A Triple Silica Jump.

The dancer landed perfectly.

A ripple of excited whispers echoed around the stage and the strangest thing happened. The sand sprites' wings fluttered and the dunes began to sing out a strong and hopeful sound like a cry of joy. All eyes looked towards the dunes and when they turned again to the stage, the dancer had disappeared.

Cassie barely remembered finishing the ballet with the other sand dancers, nor hearing the rapturous applause of the audience afterwards. As soon as she could, she walked off stage and rushed into the darkness to find the dancer. Cassie found a dropped scarf at the side of the stage, and headed up the nearby dune.

There, at the top, stood the dancer.

Cassie stopped suddenly, feeling very shy. She took a few tentative footsteps closer, and could see her mother's face.

'Your dancing was beautiful,' Cassie told Marina. 'I have never seen a Triple Silica Jump before. You made it look so easy.'

Marina smiled. 'It is very tiring. Come closer. I can feel a strange tingling in my heart that can only mean one thing. Cassie!'

Silence.

Cassie's throat was very dry. 'Yes,' she whispered, and before she had even finished saying the word, she found herself wrapped up in her mother's arms and being held tightly.

'Oh, Cassie, do you know how long I have dreamed of this moment? Ever since I left I have thought about you constantly. But I need you to know that it was necessary. I would never have gone if it wasn't imperative that I . . .' She faltered, afraid to say too much.

'It's all right,' Cassie told her. 'Last term I discovered the reason that you had been away. That you had to go to save the dunes.'

'But I thought it was to be kept a secret,' said Marina.

'It was and it is, but I had to find out what had happened to you and I . . . went snooping,' Cassie admitted.

'Sounds like the Marramgrass spirit to me,' Marina said, smiling. 'I am relieved that you know the real reason.'

Cassie looked up at her mother's face bathed in moonlight. It was not quite as she had remembered it all those years ago and yet it was familiar. There was tiredness about her face, and a few lines had appeared, but her smile was exactly the same.

'I have been travelling for so long and it is good to be back.' Marina stroked Cassie's cheek. 'Oh, Cassie, Cassie, more than anything I want to hear all about what has been happening to you over the years.'

'Where shall I begin? Shall I start with now and work backwards or go the other way around?'

Marina laughed and held Cassie's hand as they began to walk towards the school. 'I really don't mind as long as I get to hear about everything.'

Cassie thought for a moment. 'I will start with the moment when Aunt Euphorbia found me after the Great Storm.'

'Did she teach you to dance?'

Cassie pulled a face and said, 'Aunt Euphorbia always told me that she didn't know anything about dancing, apart from the fact that it causes nothing but misery and heartbreak.'

'I thought she might have a change of heart. She was once a very fine dancer,' Marina said softly.

'So Lexie was right. She was convinced that Aunt Euphorbia must have once loved dancing. But what about you? You must have had some adventures, travelling the dunes of the world learning all the different dance steps.'

Marina paused. 'Some adventures, but a lot of hard slog too!'

Cassie smiled. 'Have you got all the information about the dune dances that you need?' she asked. It was such a big question that it almost dried up in Cassie's mouth.

Before Marina could reply, she froze and looked like she was listening hard. She scooped her long cloak around Cassie and they both shrank down behind a rock until voices and footsteps passed by.

'I am not ready to be discovered yet,' she whispered. 'I want a bit more time with my baby.'

'I am not a baby,' Cassie said petulantly.

'You'll always be my baby. Do you remember how you used to wait up for me?' Marina asked.

'And you would dance for me until I went back to sleep.'

Her mother hugged her very tightly. 'You must be exhausted after performing in the ballet. I was so proud of you.'

Those words made Cassie's heart glow and her wings tremble. Her mother, the prima dune dancer, was back in her rightful place. Her friend Rubus had also returned. The Blue Moon Ballet had gone well. She felt certain that Madame Rosa would forgive her, and she would be allowed to stay at the dance school. In spite of their original intentions, it seemed that Lysander and his mother had not passed on their secrets. Perhaps Madame Rosa might even let him join the dance school! For the first time she felt she truly understood what Madame Rosa had meant when she'd told them, *When you find your place in the world it is truly a beautiful moment.*

Cassie and her mother walked along the shadows of the beach in silence. They did not notice the dark clouds that were gathering on the horizon. They were enjoying each other's company and the feel of the other's hand in theirs, until the blue moon's light merged into the pale yellow of an early morning sun.

My mum was taking part in a research project on sand dunes and she took me and my little sister, Edie, along. One night a humming noise woke us up and Edie wanted to go to the toilet, so we crept out of the tent. We lay on our tummies to watch the full moon and it was then that we saw them. A group of tiny creatures in a circle of light. They wore beautiful shimmering costumes and they were dancing to the most beautiful music we had ever heard. My mum says that we must have been dreaming, but we know we weren't and so do you!

Isobel, Beatrix and Cassandra Edith Barr, 2010